# DEDUCTIVE CIGAR REASONING

"The ashes indicate this was not a hurried killing. So that would rule out this being a robbery."

"How do you figure that?"

"Stan had smoked almost half of his Churchill. That'd take about twenty minutes. The length of both the ashes are about the same. That puts Stan sitting across this desk from the other man talking with him, each smoking a Montecristo Churchill for at the very least twenty minutes. That's when Rupert laid his cigar in the ashtray, the butt pointed in his direction, and stood up. The killer set his cigar down, too, leaving the same length ash in the tray, got up, went behind Rupert, and did the deed. The body dropped sideways, landing where it is."

"So Rupert must have trusted him."

"Enough to give him a cigar and chat for twenty minutes."

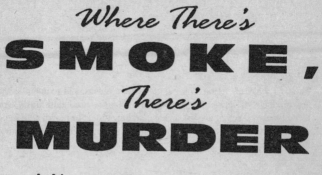

# Where There's SMOKE, There's MURDER

A Nicholas Chase Cigar Mystery

## HARRY PAUL LONSDALE

AVON TWILIGHT

This is a work of fiction. Names, characters, places, and incidents either are products of the author's imagination or are used fictitiously. Any resemblance to actual events, locales, organizations, or persons, living or dead, is entire coincidental and beyond the intent of either the author or the publisher.

AVON BOOKS, INC.
1350 Avenue of the Americas
New York, New York 10019

Copyright © 1999 by H. Paul Jeffers
Inside cover author photo by Kevin Gordon
Published by arrangement with the author
Library of Congress Catalog Card Number: 98-91014
ISBN: 0-380-80298-8
**www.avonbooks.com/twilight**

First Avon Twilight Printing: April 1999

AVON TWILIGHT TRADEMARK REG. U.S. PAT. OFF. AND IN OTHER COUNTRIES, MARCA REGISTRADA, HECHO EN U.S.A.

Printed in the U.S.A.

WCD 10 9 8 7 6 5 4 3 2 1

For Johnny

**Try one of the proprietor's cigars.**

Sherlock Holmes
*The Bruce-Partington Plans*

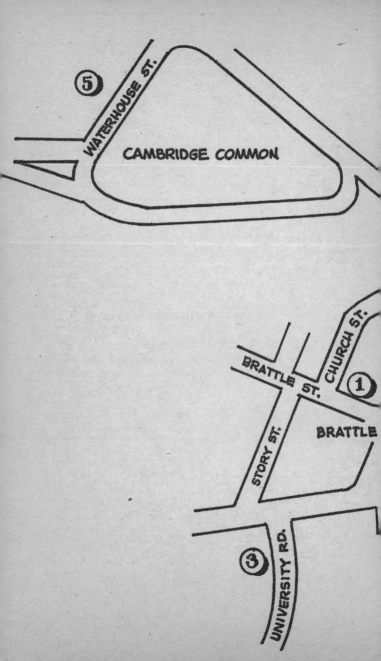

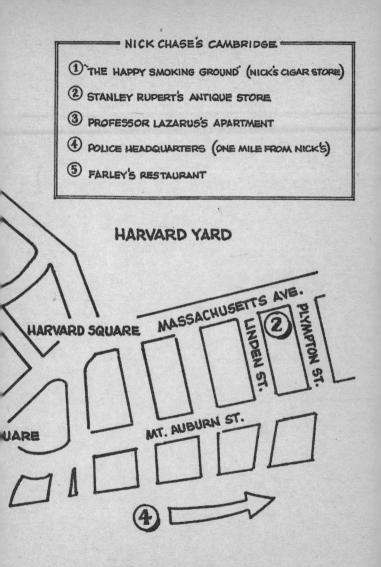

# PART I

## Cuffs to Coronas

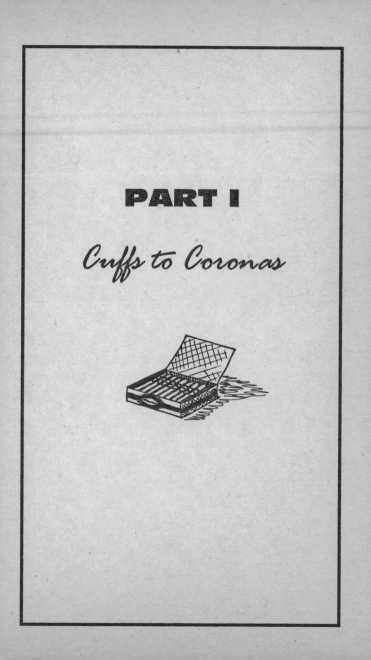

# Prologue

To THE RIGHT of the white door stood a man-size bare-chested figure with fringed buckskin leggings, brightly beaded belt with a sheathed knife, moccasins, and multi-colored feather headdress. The right arm of this fanciful American Indian rose in a graceful arc. The hand, forming a kind of salute, shielded squinting black eyes. The cupped left hand cradled a bundle of wooden cigars.

Six months after this artifact of American merchandising had been set up in front of the store, the Indian vanished, purloined by stealth in the dead of night.

In its place Nick Chase had found a hand-printed note:

*We have your Indian. He will be returned unharmed upon delivery at high noon tomorrow to the foot of the statue of John Harvard a box of twenty-five superior cigars. These cigars must be suitable to the elevated stature of the survivors of a brutal testing of the mettle of a blessed band of men who are likely to be this nation's political leaders in the decades to come.*

*WARNING! Inferior cigars will be an invitation to a calamitous outcome.*

Assigned to investigate the theft, Detective Jack Lerch of the Cambridge police force asked Nick, ''Did you see a movie some years ago about Harvard Law School students called *The Paper Chase*?''

''The only movie I remember seeing about Harvard,'' Nick said impatiently, ''was a sappy thing called *Love Story*.''

''I believe *The Paper Chase* was also a book before being made into a film. The law professor in it was played by John Houseman. This was before he made TV commercials for a Wall Street firm. If you'd seen the movie you would have learned that the first year of law at Harvard is quite arduous. Those who complete it in real life have been known to want to blow off a little steam. I think your Indian was just too tempting a target. The leader of these bandits probably passed your store every day on the way to class. I venture to say he could even be one of your regular customers.''

After pondering this for a moment, Nick gave a quick nod. ''You may be right. I know a young man I could nominate as a very likely suspect.''

''I remember when I was kid,'' Lerch went on, ''I phoned places that sold cigarettes, tobacco, and cigars and asked if they had Prince Albert in a can. If the answer was yes I would yell, 'Well, let him out.' The taking of your Indian was probably the same sort of thing.''

''On a somewhat larger and more daring scale,'' Nick said.

''Of course, I appreciate how you must feel about the theft, you being an ex-cop, so if you decide to press charges . . .''

Having pulled the Prince Albert-in-a-can joke himself, Nick said, ''Forget it. I'll just let this silliness play out.''

With cigars delivered as demanded, the Indian reappeared two nights later. Attached by tape to the hand holding the bundle of cigars was an envelope containing a postal money order for the cost of the cigars.

Reporting this by phone to Lerch, Nick laughed. ''This was a pretty dumb gang of kidnappers, wouldn't you agree? One of these guys literally signed his name to the crime.''

''If you want to prosecute I can pick him up,'' Lerch

replied. "Of course, a felony conviction will rule out a career in law for this poor guy."

Rather than being redeemed, the money order had been framed and displayed on the wall behind the sales counter, to be joined by thirteen others in as many years.

Also framed on the wall was an original copy of the world's most famous poem on cigars, "The Betrothed." In the handwriting of its author, Rudyard Kipling, it began:

> *Open the old cigar-box, get me a Cuba stout,*
> *For things are running crossways,*
> *and Maggie and I are out.*

Describing Maggie's demand that he choose between marrying her and continuing to smoke cigars, it concluded with:

> *A million surplus Maggies*
> *are willing to bear the yoke;*
> *And a woman is only a woman,*
> *but a good cigar is a Smoke.*
> *Light me another Cuba:*
> *I hold to me first-sworn vows,*
> *If Maggie will have no rival,*
> *I'll have no Maggie for spouse!*

Lest a passerby on the north side of Brattle Street miss the meaning of the traditional wooden icon of the American tobacco seller, a three-sided bay window displayed products for sale within. And an engraved bronze plaque to the left of the white door provided conclusive testimony to the nature of the business transacted by the proprietor:

> *No less true, and set aside all joke,*
> *From oldest time he ever dealt in smoke;*
> *His capital all smoke, smoke all his store,*
> *'Twas nothing else; but lovers ask no more—*
> *And thousands enter daily at his door.*

Above the entrance, raised gold-leaf letters on a dark
green background proclaimed:

## THE HAPPY SMOKING GROUND
*Always the Finest in Cigars, Tobacco, Pipes*

Should a patron wish to know the particulars of the
owner and how it happened that he had established such a
store, he could obtain the answer by examining another
item hung on the wall behind the cash register. Adjacent to
the fourteen postal money orders was the framed cover and
three pages from a nine-year-old edition of *Cigar Smoker*.

The magazine was noted for covers featuring celebrities
with a cigar in hand or mouth; its debut issue in the spring
of 1980 had featured W. C. Fields, followed in June by
Arnold Schwarzenegger, the late Orson Welles in Septem-
ber, and in the Christmas edition movie actress Meg Holly
in a floppy Santa Claus hat. Subsequent years had featured
a glittery roster of stellar names in popular culture. Yet for
the magazine's tenth anniversary the figure on the magazine
cover had on the dress blue uniform of a lieutenant of the
New York Police Department.

Why the publication had chosen to put Nick Chase on
its cover had been suggested in the accompanying headline:

## CUFFS TO CORONAS
*Cigar Smoker*'s Latest Hall of Famer
Went From Top Cop to Premier Cigarist

The article inside had pointed out Nicholas Chase had
been a tall, flat-bellied, lion-maned, hard homicide detective
with a square no-nonsense jaw and tight street-smart half
smile with a cigar jutting from it like an accusing finger.
Back then the detective of the NYPD's murder squad had
been the sharpest sleuth to stalk shadowy streets of a great
metropolis since Sherlock Holmes first donned a deerstalker
hat to shake Dr. John H. Watson from sound slumber with
'The game is afoot.'

"Some ten years later," the article went on, "Nick is

still six feet two, but his weight has gone from 195 pounds to 215 and his belt size has expanded from 38 to 42. The mane is thinner and silver-gray. Sleek three-piece suits tailored by Brooks Brothers, which he wore in New York City during his police career, have been replaced by cardigan sweaters, color-coordinated trousers, and tweed jackets with suede elbow patches chosen for maximum comfort rather than to provide room for a detective's shoulder holster and snubbed-nose .38-caliber revolver.''

What had not changed, noted the article, was Nick's passion for cigars. Nor had he abandoned the brand he smoked as a dapper crime buster. It was an H. Upmann Lonsdale. But the 1962 American embargo on imports from Communist Cuba forced Nick to switch from Havana-mades to those rolled by exiles in the Dominican Republic.

Another difference between the Nick Chase of the 1960s and the 1990s was where he obtained his Lonsdales. As a cop he had bought them a few at a time in Nat Sherman's store in Manhattan. Now he kept boxes of them in stock in his own store on historic Brattle Street in Cambridge, Massachusetts.

Readers of the magazine profile learned he had been born in 1934 in Brooklyn and had joined the New York Police Department after graduating from high school in 1952. Married in 1960 to a beauty named Maggie Singleton, he became a father in 1961. His son was named Kevin. Daughter Jean was born in 1967. Maggie died of cancer in 1969.

Promoted to the rank of detective in 1962, Nick had spent the next twenty years working homicides. Shot in the hip and relegated to desk duty, he retired with a full pension and a disability allowance the next year. Bored and tired of puttering around in a garden at the back of his house in New Rochelle, New York, he used his savings, proceeds of Maggie's life insurance policy, and funds from the sale of the New Rochelle house to lease the building on Brattle Street.

A few blocks from Harvard University, The Happy Smoking Ground soon ranked in the cigar industry's yearly survey as one of the top five small cigar stores in the United States. This had been why *Cigar Smoker* chose to add him to its "Cigar Hall of Fame" and put his photo on the cover.

With the honor had come a lifetime free subscription to the magazine and an impressively weighty bronze plaque that now hung next to a frame that held his gold NYPD detective shield.

Kept in a drawer was the Smith & Wesson .38 police special revolver he bought on the day he had received the shield.

Though he had never been compelled to fire it, he had been forced to draw it four times. The last was the instant before he was shot by a young man who had then been cut down by the guns of other detectives. The youth had not survived long enough to learn that his bullet succeeded in killing a career. Had it not, Nick would not have left the police force, not become bored with his retirement, not decided to move close to his children, not gotten the idea to open a cigar store, and not been able, as he peered beyond the wooden Indian, to note the unusual appearance on Brattle Street early on a Monday morning of the man who had sold him the Kipling poem.

# One

STANLEY RUPERT'S SUNDAY had begun badly and gotten worse as it wore on.

First, while anticipating a couple of leisurely hours in the delightful company of Roger Woolley examining a new exhibition of Theodore Roosevelt letters and diaries in the Widener Library, he had been accosted by Jerome Lazarus.

With gaunt face as pale as death and scarecrow-thin arms flailing he had dashed across the foyer to the grand staircase below John Singer Sargent's *World War Murals*, shouting as he approached, "Stanley, it's urgent I speak to you."

"Can't you see Woolley and I are about to do the Roosevelt exhibit? Come to the shop at four o'clock. There's nothing that can't wait. Now please go away and leave Woolley and me to see the Roosevelt show in peace."

Turning aside, Lazarus said dejectedly, "I only hope four o'clock won't be too late."

Clearly stunned and embarassed, Woolley waited until Lazarus was gone and said, "I think you ought to talk with him now, Stan. He's terribly upset."

"Nonsense! This is another case of Lazarus proving that a Ph.D. after a man's name doesn't prevent him from making himself a jackass. He seems to become more bizarre day by day, and giving up smoking has only made him worse."

The Roosevelt papers, though cleverly arranged, had offered nothing worth more than a few minutes of lively discussion during a stroll to brunch at the Cambridge Hyatt Regency at a table with a splendid view of the Charles River. But two hours later as he and Woolley crossed Harvard Square he had seen an apparition that stopped him cold in his tracks.

"Stan, you look positively dreadful," Woolley exclaimed. "Are you ill?" Characteristically assuming the worse, he asked, "Is it your heart?"

Rather than explain the reason for that moment of alarm he lied. "My heart is perfect. It's indigestion. I shouldn't have had the clams for lunch." And with that, he and Woolley parted company.

Then four o'clock came and went without Lazarus keeping their appointment. When telephone calls to Lazarus's apartment proved unavailing, he had driven to Lazarus's address, saw no lights in his apartment's windows, and continued on to his own Victorian house on Cowperthwaite Street. When his phone rang he answered in expectation of hearing Lazarus's voice, only to have to listen to another pleading harrangue, the third in a week.

After hanging up he secured doors and windows downstairs, turned on the lights of front and back entrances, and retreated to his bedroom. Leaving the door ajar to see the shadow should anyone move along the corridor, he positioned his reading chair to face the door and settled down with a Luger pistol in his lap.

Looking around the bedroom, he found the walls lined with shelves of books concerning the dubious history of mankind. But he also found the record of his own lengthy and eventful life: framed pictures of a baby in his mother's arms, bow-tied schoolboy with a forced smile in formal pose while in the sixth grade, a self-conscious, self-doubting teenager in ill-fitting tuxedo beside a girl who had been his senior prom date, whose name six decades had erased from his memory.

Beside these innocent moments of his life was a portrait of a sad woman trapped in a failing marriage entered into during the war. Next to this, photos of the daughter she had been forced to raise alone: Millicent as a child and on the day her father did not show up to give her hand in marriage, and Millie's son Rex at age four, now grown into young manhood.

A slightly-out-of-focus snapshot taken the year before his younger brother Norman's untimely death showed Stanley, Norman, and Norman's son Harry in front of a Las Vegas casino, proving the saying that the acorns do not fall far from the oaks.

A camera had caught Harry's future uncle and the youth who would be Rex's grandfather near war's end with Lazarus, Sid Gold, and Johnny Little. Though helmeted and unshaven, they looked like boys playing a game of soldiers who deserved spankings by their fathers for smoking the cigars jutting from their cocky smirks. A second photo taken on the deck of Lazarus's seaside retreat showed the quartet a few years older, but even more smug because they had by a twist of history become wealthy beyond their richest dreams.

" 'Oh what a tangled web we weave,' " he muttered as his eyes shifted anxiously from the pictures on the wall toward the door, " 'when first we practice to deceive.' "

Yet, Stanley thought, as Matthew Arnold had observed, history was a great Mississippi of falsehood. But not all the charlatans set their hands to writing. Stuart Mosley willfully twisted historical facts to suit theory in a paper proven more fraudulent than scholarly; George Dickson brazenly thought he could engage Stanley's expertise to swindle the entire world of fine art.

By exposing them he had validated Nietzsche, adopted doctrinaire of the Nazis, who espoused in *The Twilight of the Idols* that history amounted to nothing more than the belief in the senses, the belief in falsehood. Watching the doorway, he wondered if he might have been fooled by his own senses while crossing Harvard Square. Could what he thought he had seen really been, as he told Woolley, the clams at lunch? Had belly tricked eyes?

After long hours with neither flesh nor an avenging spirit appearing in the hallway, he got out of the chair, carried the heavy Luger to a window, and peered between the slanted roofs of nearby houses and beyond them to the black swath of Memorial Drive that would soon bustle with cars of the morning rush taking people to jobs in Cambridge and Boston.

Beyond the cities' geographic divider in pale and tenuous first light, the view of the Charles River seemed to be the handiwork of a superb landscape painter. Soon a slender figure in a racing scull spoiled the illusion. Bringing life to the scene and looking like a black water spider, the combined silhouettes of rower and boat left a meager wake that lengthened and widened in a V so shallow that it dissolved before touching either shore.

As he turned away from the window, a movement near the open door caused him to leap back with fright. Jerking up his arm and pointing the pistol, he realized the movement had been himself reflected in the glass showcase that protected his collection of antique cigar boxes.

Eyes drifting down from his backward image settled upon a mahogany humidor. Smiling, he laid the gun beside it and stroked the box tenderly, for nothing in his life had ever proved quite so effective in dispelling his anxieties, both real and mistaken, as opening it, selecting a cigar, lighting it, and then losing himself in eddying drifts of clouds of smoke.

Throughout the history of the five centuries since Europeans had been introduced to cigars by the natives of the Western hemisphere, every aspect of smoking tobacco had been construed as a metaphor. To smoke was to recognize in the ash and in the smoke itself the transitory nature of life, for what was the fate of man but to flare up for a time and then burn out?

Sir Walter Raleigh, he recalled, had bet Queen Elizabeth I he could weigh the smoke of his pipe. When the bemused monarch took him up on the wager, he began by weighing his fully packed pipe. He then smoked it until only a little ash remained in the bowl and placed the pipe on the scale again. The difference in the weights, he claimed, was the weight of the smoke.

It was a trick that could not have worked had Sir Walter tried it with a cigar. Smoke tobacco in a pipe, and the pipe is left intact and tangible. A cigar vanishes with its smoke.

Lifting the humidor's gleaming mahogany lid in anticipation of dispersing shadows of haunted memory and a
disturbing vision that had not vanished like cigar smoke
during the long vigilant night, he found the cedar-lined box
empty. Ordinarily this would have meant sending his assistant to fetch two or three boxes from his private locker
in Nick Chase's humidor room. But as he gazed into the
box, sinking disappointment quickly gave way to soaring
inspiration. The key to the problems of his troubling Sunday, he realized, was to visit The Happy Smoking Ground
himself.

Consequently, two hours after the sun rose over the cities
flanking the Charles, he passed with the indifference of
years of familiarity Nick Chase's wooden Indian and poetic
plaque, dashed under the green sign, and stepped into the
store.

# Two

WITH AN UNLIT Upmann in the right corner of his lips, Nick had on a brown-and-white houndstooth sport jacket with tan suede patches at the elbows. Left unbuttoned, it revealed a chocolate-toned sleeveless cardigan sweater whose large faux bone buttons strained against a bulge of belly as the avuncular wearer leaned with his arms folded atop a hand-cranked bronze cash register. Discovered by Nick in Rupert's antiques store, it stood on the wooden top of a glass display case that was crammed with the gadgetry and other indispensable implements and accoutrements of tobacco smoking, though primarily for the requisite rituals of enjoying fine cigars.

"All right, Chase," Rupert demanded in a surprisingly deep voice that conveyed as much determination as his stride, "where are my Montecristos? You said I could have them Monday. That's today." A bony finger wagged threateningly. "You had better not tell me they haven't come in yet."

"Fresh off the plane from Santo Domingo on Saturday afternoon, Stan," Nick answered. "I sent Sam Gargan out to Logan Airport specifically to pick them up. I was about to put your six in your locker. I expected your assistant to come in for them."

"I decided to do it myself," Rupert huffed as a hand plunged into a pocket of a blue pinstriped suit for his wallet. "I shall take two boxes now and leave the rest in the locker. The delivery came in the nick of time. Pardon the pun! When I was forced to offer a cigar to a dinner companion, I thought I had one left in my bedroom humidor, but didn't. I had wasted my last cigar on a scoundrel. If he knew as little of rare documents as he did about cigars I would have skinned him, instead of the other way round."

Nick patted his belly and barked a laugh that jiggled the Upmann. "Stanley Rupert, king of trade in antiquities and ephemera of history, *skinned*? That'll be the day!"

"The antiques trade is not like cigars," Rupert said while hundred-dollar bills came out of the wallet and landed on top of the counter. "You could never slap a gold-and-black Cohiba band on a cheap Mexican stogie and expect to get away with passing it off as a prized handmade Havana, could you? One puff and you'd be found out. Not so with the detritus of history. You have no idea how slick forgers are, and not only in antiques."

"You're right about that, Stanley," Nick said as he cranked a handle to open the register's drawer. "I spent two years on the bunco squad and was a total flop. I just couldn't feel the old adrenaline pumping in excitement about my arresting anyone whose criminal imagination was limited to simple thievery by deception. For me, the measure of felonious accomplishment will always be a murder. I'm talking about premeditated homicide. A mystery that requires a bit of detective work."

"I know one forger who was so accustomed to writing Abraham Lincoln's signature," Rupert said, "that he once signed one of his own bank checks 'A. Lincoln.' And a stupid clerk *cashed it.*"

Nick slammed the register drawer shut, turned, and entered a long cool room lined with rows of private lockers and floor-to-ceiling glass shelves stacked with cigar boxes.

"So, Stan, what was it that you bought that was worth parting with a Montecristo Churchill?"

Following Nick into the room, Rupert chuckled, "It's an item related to cigars that is as valuable and genuine as the Kipling poem I sold you. I also expect to let this unique item pass to you with only a very modest markup for myself.'' His voice went to a whisper. "Christopher Columbus. A diary page! Dated October 12, 1492! Written in the admiral's quarters aboard the *Santa Maria*. It details Columbus's first experience with *cigarros*.''

"As I recall,'' Nick replied, taking down from the shelf the six boxes of Montecristos and placing them on a small table, "Chris didn't enjoy the experience.''

"The diary page is ideal for framing,'' Rupert said, taking a key to his private locker from a pocket as Nick left him alone. Emerging from the walk-in humidor a few moments later with two of the boxes cradled in the crook of his left albow, he asked, "When do you shut up your shop today, Nick?''

"Eight o'clock on Mondays.''

"Then I shall expect you in my office at eight-fifteen.''

# Three

WITH THE UNEXPECTED customer gone, Nick removed the band of his Upmann, took a brass trimmer from his jacket pocket, cut the cigar, and held it between the thumb and forefinger of the left hand. With a burning long wooden match in the right he barely touched the cigar with the flame then turned the cigar and blew lightly on the blackened end, causing the tobacco to flare evenly around. Satisfied that it was properly lighted, he extinguished the match with a flick of his wrist.

Putting the cigar in his mouth, he wondered about Rupert's very peculiar behavior and savored the first of the day's smokes.

By the closing of the store at eight o'clock, if the past proved to be prologue, he would burn up part of the day's profits to the extent of six Upmanns. But thanks to an unexpected early purchase of six boxes of Montecristos, the tally of the cash in the drawer of the clanky old register already accounted for more money than he normally would have expected to take in during the entire day.

Always slow, Monday mornings were ideal for checking the account books and reviewing inventory in the display cases of the store itself and the stocks of the most popular brands on shelves in the walk-in humidor.

Consequently he was occupied there when he heard the

white door open and a familiar voice bellowing, "This is a stickup."

Stepping from the humidor, he found the dumpy, balding, and profusely perspiring figure of Dick Levitan in an electric-blue jogging suit. "I'm busy now. Can you come back later?"

Levitan wiped his face with a sleeve. "How much later?"

"We're open till eight on Mondays. In the meantime, can I interest you in purchasing a cigar?"

Levitan leaned on the counter. "Do you sell cheap ones?"

"Sorry."

"What about used? Or, as I am required to say in commercial copy for automobiles, previously owned?"

"A job for which you get paid extremely well."

"Only as long as the ratings stay up. The only way of making a living that's more lucrative than being on the radio is cigar store owner. A box of twenty-five of my usual Arturo Fuente Flor Finas will get me through a week of broadcasts."

"It never occurred to me in these antismoking, politically correct times that the station lets you smoke in the studio."

"As long as I keep the ratings up," Levitan said as Nick returned to the humidor for the cigars, "they have no choice."

At ten o'clock Peg Baron burst through the door. Barely taller than the length of the black cello case in her right hand, she breathlessly exclaimed, "Nick, darling, if a crisis is to be averted I must have a certain brand of cigars *immediately*."

Nick emerged from the humidor. "When did you start smoking?"

Propping the cello against the counter, she brushed back a wayward strand of hair that a little touching up had maintained as auburn as it had been when he had met her, longer ago than he could recall, or she cared to. "They are for Wilhelm Wieder, the world's freshest interpreter of Tchaikovsky's first piano concerto. He's a mere twenty-six-year-old who exploded onto the European concert stage three years ago. He begins a series of recitals and concerts in the Boston area with his long-awaited American debut tonight with the BSO. If that weren't enough pressure, he's out of his favorite cigars and will not rehearse until he's provided with the kind he smokes. I can't overestimate the seriousness of this crisis.''

Nick took his cigar from his mouth. ''What kind does this postpubescent prodigy piano-player prefer?''

Ignoring the goading disrespect, she plopped a brown purse on the counter. ''I jotted it down. It has a Spanish name.''

''Cigars generally do.'' Taking a note from her, he let out a grunt. ''All the world, it seems, smokes Montecristo today.''

''Beg pardon?''

''Not two hours ago I sold six boxes to Stanley Rupert.''

Alarm clouded her expression. ''Does that mean you're *out*?''

''Not to worry,'' he said, gently laying the Upmann into an ashtray as long as the cigar. ''I just got in a fresh supply.''

''Wasn't that rather an early hour for Stanley Rupert to be up and about?'' she asked. ''He usually doesn't open his temple of the past till one o'clock.''

''When a man wants his favorite smoke,'' said Nick, picking up his cigar and admiring its lengthening, fragile gray ash, ''the hours weigh very heavily.''

''I wouldn't know.''

''Of course you wouldn't,'' Nick said, gazing at the Kipling poem. '' 'A woman is just a woman, but—' ''

Exasperation glinting in her green eyes cut him off. ''Will you *please* get a move on? Time is of the essence.''

Putting the cigar back in the ashtray and backing away from the counter, he held up defensive hands. ''Evidently Stan Rupert isn't the only person up and out early this morning with a bee buzzing around in one's bonnet.''

With a sigh and an anxious look at her watch, she pleaded, ''These cigars and I are already overdue at Symphony Hall. The rehearsal was supposed to start at nine o'clock.''

Nick entered the humidor. "Since when have you been designated the Boston Symphony Orchestra's errand girl? Or should I say errand *person*?''

"By the way. I'll have to pay for these cigars later.''

"The kid sends you out to get cigars that run three hundred dollars a box,'' Nick said, stepping from the humidor with the two boxes, "and he doesn't give you money or a credit card?''

"He didn't send me. I got an urgent phone call this morning from the manager of the symphony office. Because he knows that I know a man who owns a cigar store, he just assumed it would be easy for me to get the cigars. How could I refuse?''

"Anything and everything for the sake of music.''

Peg scooped up the boxes. "By the way, I just happen to have an extra ticket for tonight's concert. If you would care to use it we could have late supper at Farley's. It will be my treat. You can get Sam to close up the store.''

"Monday night is when young Mr. Gargan has a seminar.''

"Professor Woolley? Craig Spencer?''

"Woolley is working on a novel. Craig is out of town for at least a month. But it wouldn't matter who closed the shop. I am otherwise engaged this evening.''

She made a sour face. "A hockey game, no doubt.''

"This evening while you and the Symphony Hall crowd are all lost in the rapture of Tchaikovsky as interpreted by the whiz kid, I will be finding out exactly what it was that rousted our mutual friend Stanley from bed so early on a Monday morning.''

"I thought you said he came in for cigars.''

"I've known Stan fifteen profitable years. He never smokes before noon, so his Montecristos could have waited. I suspect he wants to see me about something else that's on his mind.''

"Good gravy, Nick,'' she said, shaking her head as she placed the box of cigars under one arm while holding the cello with the other, "you always have a way of making life so mysterious."

"You mean it isn't?"

"As Freud said, 'Sometimes a cigar is just a cigar.'"

# Four

As Nick stood in the door watching Peg wave her arms at an approaching taxi, a voice with the throaty rasp of a man who had clocked the passage of more than half of his seven decades by emptying too many tumblers of bourbon declared, "It's none of my business, Nick, but don't you agree that it is about time you married that sweet lady?"

Turning as Peg entered the taxi, Nick faced a figure that seemed to him as stately as the mast of the *U.S.S. Constitution*, moored beside a dock in Boston Harbor for examination by tourists and hordes of students taken there on outings by junior high school history teachers.

With a smile for Roger Woolley, himself a retired teacher of history and the man who had sold him the property that housed his store, on condition he be allowed to continue to reside in a small apartment on the top floor, Nick answered, "You are right about that, Professor."

Adjusting his hold on a walking stick topped by a hound's head in silver, Woolley beamed. "I'm delighted to hear it!"

"It is none of your business."

"Very well," said Woolley, stroking a gray Van Dyke beard. "I'll marry her."

"You could do a lot worse."

"Of course, you'd have to be my best man."

Nick held the door open for him. "I consider it an honor to have been asked."

"It's honor by default, my friend," said Woolley, entering the store and inhaling the redolent rich aroma of tobacco. "Men on whom I might have bestowed it, if I had ever gotten around to taking a bride, are deceased."

"Not all of them, surely."

"It is one of the bittersweet realities of being old, as you shall discover when you reach my age," Woolley said with a sigh as he inspected the boxes of cigars in a display case just inside the entrance, "that all the personages of your own generation are either buried or are about to be."

"Well, there's a sweet prospect," Nick said, closing the door. "Thank you very much."

"It used to be that the first thing I'd read in the *Globe* was the front page," Woolley continued as he proceeded deeper into the store. "Now I turn immediately to the obituaries to see whose funeral I'll be going to."

"None on tap today, I hope."

"As a rule, people aren't buried on Mondays. It's usually an event reserved for Wednesdays and Saturdays."

"I hadn't noticed."

"I suppose it's because the pastors of churches need a day or two to tally the proceeds of their Sunday collection boxes. Or maybe it's because funeral directors—in my day they were called undertakers—want weekends off. Perhaps it's that gravediggers, who have to work Saturdays, belong to a labor union that demands its members get two days off in a row. Who knows?"

"I certainly don't."

"There was a moment yesterday when I was afraid I would be witnessing another burial."

"Whose?"

In his procession through the store, Woolley had reached a wall taken up entirely by an astonishing display of briar pipes. "So simple a device," he muttered, "yet such a lovely variety of sizes and shapes to choose from."

"You're in the market for a new pipe?"

Woolley turned and sighed forlornly. "Alas, my favorite old meerschaum slipped from my grasp last night and shattered on the tiles of the bathroom floor. Quite beyond repair, I'm afraid.''

"I see," said Nick, consolingly. "That explains the macabre tone. The death of a pipe is a terrible thing."

"There's an old poem. Perhaps you know it:

> *Ah! what would the world be to us*
> *Tobaccoless?—Fearful bore!*
> *We would dread the day after tomorrow*
> *Worse than the day before.''*

"You should have been a professor of poetry, not history.''

"I found the ode in an old book. The author was cited as 'Wrongfellow,' a play on Henry Wadsworth *Long*fellow, whose grave is not far from here.''

"I've visited it.''

Woolley lifted a black bent briar with meerschaum-lined bowl from the display. "To quote the bard of Avon on the topic:

> *Let's talk of graves, of worms, and epitaphs;*
> *Make dust our paper, and with rainy eyes*
> *Write sorrow on the bosom of the earth;*
> *Let's choose executors and talk of wills.''*

Nick chuckled. "Do I correctly deduce from this morbid mood of yours this morning that the alter ago of your retirement, the pseudonymous Matthew Mark, is at work on another mystery novel?''

"You do.''

"I trust the brilliant but quirky Inspector Jake Elwell is well on his way to figuring out who done it.''

"The inspector is damn well *not*.''

"Well, I have every confidence he soon will be.''

Woolley weighed the handsome pipe in his right hand. "Did you know that Shakespeare was a pipe smoker? There is a story, probably apochryphal, that Will smoked tobacco in company with Francis Bacon and Sir Walter Raleigh himself. It was in a house in Durham from which they watched the boats on the Thames and discussed the highest themes of poetry and science. I like this pipe very much.''

"Then take it with you. Consider it my gift."

"Certainly not!"

"A present in anticipation of your wedding."

With a twinkle in his eyes, Woolley mouthed the pipe at a rakish angle. "You asked about the funeral I thought I might be attending."

"I believe I did."

"Yesterday I feared Stan Rupert was having a heart attack."

"Obviously he wasn't."

Woolley's eyes went wide. "How could you possibly know that?"

"He was in here a little while ago to pick up a fresh supply of Montecristo Churchills. He wants to see me this evening at his store. He says he has acquired a page from Christoper Columbus's diary and he expects to sell it to me."

Woolley tapped the glass countertop with the head of his walking stick. "Utterly impossible. The only extant Columbus diary is in a museum in Spain." He paused, stroking his beard and thinking. "This spurious claim of Stan to have a page from it was obviously a ruse to meet with you privately on his own turf."

Nick grinned knowingly. "Of course it was."

## Five

WITH THE WHITE door locked precisely at eight o'clock Nick tenderly stroked the stoic Indian's wooden shoulder. Pausing a moment, he heard the faint sound of Woolley's typewriter floating down from the third floor. Looking in every direction from The Happy Smoking Ground to Brattle Square, he saw the routine and humdrum of everyday life.

Seeking that very thing, he had chosen to settle himself and his store in Cambridge rather than in Boston because the home of Harvard, Radcliffe, MIT, numerous other institutions of learning, and graveyards peopled by famous scholars and writers promised a peace and quiet rendered unattainable by the inroads of modernity found in the historic but restlessly growing city on the other side of the Charles. Every week, it seemed, a new skyscraper was being thrown up. Or a block of fine old houses was being demolished to clear the way for yet another off-ramp of the Massachusetts Turnpike. Or, in local parlance, the Mass Pike.

Brattle Street had been picked not only because of Roger Woolley's generous terms, but because the location offered the historic and the commercial with neither threatening to overtake and overwhelm the other. He'd preferred a place that seemed more town than city, where growing older was okay, whether it was a brick house or a human being.

Flanking his store were a discreet but handy photocopying shop and a quiet boutique dealing exclusively in women's shoes. Opposite it, a theater presenting repertory and classic films had as a neighbor a graceful house built in 1727 by William Brattle. A Colonial leader whose Tory loyalty prompted him to unwisely try to argue Cambridge citizens out of going for independence from England, he was now doomed to be remembered by all but historians primarily because of the name of a movie house, the street, and the square half a block from The Happy Smoking Ground.

Were one to walk north along Brattle, rather than toward the square, other significant addresses would be passed. At No. 76 stood the house of Samuel Longfellow, the brother of Henry, whose house was farther on, at No. 105, and whose poetry romanticized the midnight ride of Paul Revere, enshrining in America's lore and legend both silversmith and his alarming cry, "The British are coming." And at the corner of Story Street a stone marked the spot where worked a blackmsith by the name of Dexter Pratt, the "village smithy" and "mighty man" upon whom Longfellow also had bestowed immortality in another patriotic poem.

Bas relief figures of Pratt and other characters in Longfellow's works—Miles Standish, Evangeline, Hiawatha—could be seen on the Memorial Monument sculpted by Daniel Chester French in Longfellow Park. But to pay respects at the poet's grave, as Roger Woolley had noted during his macabre recitation that very morning, as well as the resting places of Oliver Wendell Holmes, James Russell Lowell, Edward Everett, Julia Ward Howe, and Henry James, you had to turn off Brattle Street and find nearby Mount Auburn Cemetery.

But as he walked south on Brattle Street toward a convergeance with Mount Auburn and Eliot Streets, not in a true square, but more in the form of a wheel, Nick's purpose was not to see the sights. After nearly fifteen years, there remained little of the historic and cultural aspects of either city on the Charles that he had not at least sampled. Therefore, as he turned from Brattle Street to walk east toward Harvard Square, the reddish brick walls of the university which lent the busy intersection its name no longer stirred within him, as they first did, the romantic images of graduates who had gone on to become great men of their times, and some for all time. Neither did he look at the faces of today's young students and search them for modern versions of the mismatched and tragic lovers in the sappy movie based on the maudlin, but best-selling, novel that contained the line, "Love means never having to say you're sorry."

More often than most people realized, Nick mused as he got to Harvard Square, to some people love meant not only not having to say you're sorry, it meant bringing it to an abrupt and violent ending. On the topic of love, George Bernard Shaw had gotten it right. When you want to read of deeds done for love, turn to the murder column. You will rarely be disappointed.

In the daily chronicling of motives for homicide that had occupied a large portion of his life, Nick recalled as he crossed the square toward Sidney Rupert's store—in Peg Baron's words, a palace of the past—love had been surpassed only by greed.

Reading 8:05 on the digital wristwatch given to him by Peg for Christmas, he assumed that she had delivered the Montecristos to the piano player, that the rehearsal had proceeded accordingly, and she and the Symphony Hall audience were at that moment either enthralled by Tchaikovsky's first piano concerto, or soon would be. Realizing he was early for his meeting with Rupert, he slowed his pace in order to arrive at the store precisely at a quarter past eight. Stopping at No. 1316, he took the measure of a competitor in the purveying of tobacco products and paraphernalia for enjoying them by examining window displays of the venerable establishment known as Leavitt & Peirce.

Finding nothing he did not offer to his own customers, he shrugged his shoulders, muttered, "A city can never have too many tobacco stores," and walked on a few paces to the windows of a bookstore. Gazing inside at the bewildering stock of new titles added since the last time he'd gone in to browse, he complimented himself on not having decided to open a bookstore, or attempted, as his daughter

Jean had proposed at the time of his retirement, to write a book about his exploits as a homicide detective.

His answer had been, "There've already been too many books by ex-cops with nothing new to say. Besides, who'd care to read a book about a detective who stupidly let some punk kid with a gun get the drop on him?"

"I would," Jean retorted saucily.

"I intend to follow the example of Melvin Purvis."

With a blank expression, she asked, "Who?"

"Purvis was the FBI agent during the 1930s who tracked down America's public enemies. He smoked a big cigar to celebrate the killing of Pretty Boy Floyd by G-men. And he used another one to signal the feds to close in for the capture of John Dillinger, who also wound up dead at Purvis's feet. But when he retired from the FBI—some say he was forced out by J. Edgar Hoover, who didn't care for Purvis getting more publicity than himself—Purvis told reporters his immediate retirement goal was to get a pipe that would hold a pound of tobacco, then find a rocking chair so he could rock and smoke. Very slowly. Now that was an ex-cop who didn't just appreciate both cigars and pipes. He kept all his priorities straight."

Instead of naming a cigar after Al Capone, someone should have named one to honor good old Melvin, thought Nick, walking on toward Rupert's address and breaking into a broad grin in anticipation of cajoling Stan into offering him one of his fresh Montecristos. Approaching the store, he found lights ablaze within, but a CLOSED sign hung in the full-length window of a black-painted door. Using a brass pocket cigar trimmer appropriately known as a guillotine, he tapped the glass twice. Unanswered, he sidestepped to a large display window.

Peering past a jumble of antique chairs, a vintage rolltop desk, and a small metal strongbox with a red "Sold" tag attached, he saw the partly open door of a storage room at the back that also served as Rupert's office.

Returning to the black front door, he knocked hard on the wood frame and waited. Unanswered, he turned the cut-glass doorknob and felt the door move. Pushing it open, he shouted, "It's me, Stan. Nick Chase."

A moment later standing in the doorway of the back room, he took his time in surveying the scene as best he could from that distance, then drew from his jacket pocket a cell phone given to him by his son Kevin and entered 911.

## Six

LOOKING PAST A litter of police cars and vans blocking one side of Massachusetts Avenue, Nick saw grim but fascinated faces corralled beyond parallel streamers of yellow POLICE LINE DO NOT CROSS tape. Gawkers, they somehow instantly materialized to see something awful and take comfort in the fact it had fallen upon someone else.

Soon reporters, photographers, and beefy youths toting TV cameras would arrive in a swarm so that citizens in much of New England might also be informed of the horror discovered in the shadow of the staid buildings of America's oldest institution of higher education. No doubt Kevin Chase would be among them, eager to obtain the gory details for readers of the *Globe*. But now the vehicle pulling to curbside was a rather ugly green, slightly battered unmarked car that to those experienced in such a tableau said the young man behind the wheel and the middle-aged one beside him were detectives.

Portly, wearing a rumpled gray suit, and exhibiting a jaunty demeanor more suitable to a Red Sox game, Sergeant John Lerch of the Cambridge PD homicide squad extended Nick a meaty hand in greeting.

Taking it, Nick said, "Evening, Jack."

"Well, my friend," Lerch said, grinning as he looked Nick up and down, "being the person who *discovered* the victim must be a first for you. And this one practically right

in the middle of Harvard Yard.'' His accent turned the venerable name into ''Havid Yad.'' With a tight smile, he
added, ''You know the first rule of homicide investigating,
Nick.''

''The person who reports discovering the body is probably the one who did the killing. It's a pretty reliable
guide.''

Lerch gently squeezed Nick's shoulder. ''Have you ever
asked yourself why it is that dead bodies are always found
either just as you sit down to dinner or at three in the
morning?''

''The policeman's lot is not an easy one, as somebody
said.''

Lerch turned to the young man who had driven the car.
''Have you met Detective Sergeant Gary Evert?''

''I haven't had the privilege,'' Nick replied.

''The privilege is mine,'' said Evert. ''I'm aware of your
reputation, sir.''

''According to the report I got on the phone at home,''
said Lerch, ''this looks like a stickup that got out of hand.''

Nick responded with a shrug. ''That's the way your first
men on the scene figure it happened.''

Lerch peered through the store window and squinted
against the bright lights beyond it. ''I gather from that dour
expression on your face you don't see it that way at all.''

Nick frowned. ''Why stick up an antiques dealer? People
who buy what Stan Rupert had for sale don't pay in cash.
They write checks. If they've got a hefty credit line, they
use plastic.''

''Maybe the killer didn't know that,'' Lerch said, rubbing a jowly jaw. ''Maybe he wasn't looking for money.
There've got to be plenty of valuable objects in there that
could be fenced. The market in heisted antiques has gotten
pretty brisk of late.''

''Things that could be stolen a whole lot easier by breaking and entering. And in the brief look I had at the crime
scene I saw nothing to support a robbery-gone-sour theory.
A stickup is usually a matter of a gun held to the head or
in the ribs. A slit throat is up close and personal.''

''That's how it happened? Geez. Nobody told me,''

Lerch said tautly. "Well, I guess you'd better come inside and show us. Then you can tell us how it happened that Nick Chase found a corpse."

"I was invited to be here."

Lerch blinked. "Say again?"

"Stanley Rupert—that's the victim—asked me to meet him here at eight-fifteen this evening."

"What for?"

"He said he had something he hoped to sell me."

"What would that be, sir?" Evert asked.

"Your courtesy is appeciated, Sergeant Evert," Nick said, touching the young man's shoulder, "but I'll feel a lot younger than I am if you'd call me Nick. The item I came to see was a page from Christopher Columbus's diary. But I never got a chance to see it. Stan was dead when I arrived."

"Dead for how long, do you think?"

"Judging from the coagulation of the blood, I'd say no more than an hour before I found the body."

"You got here at what time?"

"Eight-fifteen on the dot. When Stan didn't answer my knock I found the door unlocked. I observed the door to the office was open and went in."

"Well, let's have a look-see," said Lerch.

Entering the store, they faced a clutter of old furniture, silver and gold objects of art, decoration, or mere utility that sometime, somewhere had been the prizes of people now long dead. Items gleaned by Stanley Rupert from estate sales, musty shops in narrow byways of storied cities of Europe, stately but bankrupt country manor houses of the British Isles, and everywhere else, they spoke of Rupert's quest for profit in resaleables.

Following Nick toward the rear, Lerch was aware of glassy eyes of stuffed deer and elk heads mounted on a wall above a row of colorfully laquered boxes and chests with elaborate Oriental motifs. Meandering aisles were formed by used furniture, lamps, glass display cases, shelves of books, barrels of rusted tools, vintage weapons, trunks and crates. "This is crazy," Lerch said. "I've got junk like this in my attic."

"Don't be misled," Nick said. "When it came to the difference between trash and antiques Stanley Rupert had a shrewd eye."

The clunky but elegant cash register of The Happy Smoking Ground, he recalled, had been rescued by Rupert from a defunct grocery store Rupert had discovered and purchased, literally lock, stock, and barrel, in some crossroads village in the northernmost reaches of the piney woods of Maine.

And now in a room at the back of the store that was a jumble of things others could not carry with them into death, but the living were willing to pay dearly to own, he was sprawled facedown on a tattered and faded Oriental carpet that was probably ruined by a wide circle of congealing blood.

Keenly conscious that the man standing next to him in the doorway had been one of New York City's best homicide detectives, if not *the* best, Lerch said softly, "So, Nick. Tell us what you make of this mess."

"From here, not much."

Lerch held out an arm. "Feel free to go in."

Evert blurted, "Just be careful not to—"

"I know the drill, Sergeant," said Nick, jamming hands into his jacket pockets. "I won't touch a thing."

"No offense intended. Force of habit," Evert said.

Nick crossed the cluttered office to Rupert's surprisingly tidy desk, looked down at the top a few moments, took a deep breath, and said, "Before the victim . . ." He paused a moment to let a tightness in his throat subside. "Before he was killed he was seated at this desk with the killer on this side, facing him."

"Then how'd the body land there?" asked Lerch, pointing. "It's three feet from the desk."

"I didn't say he was killed *at* the desk," Nick said sharply. "He obviously got up at some point. Evidence that Stan and the killer sat across the desk from one another is in the ashtray."

Lerch rubbed his jaw and looked down at the large, round, glass object. "Okay. I see two mostly burned matchsticks, a half-smoked stogie, some ashes, and a cigar band.''

"Long matches made for lighting cigars," Nick said. "And the ashes of *two* cigars."

"I see only one butt," said Evert.

"*Two* cigars were smoked. Rupert clipped his with a guillotine. You can see the cut-off portion in the tray. Because there is just the one, I would say the second smoker used a punch instead of a clipper to open the end of his."

"If you say so, Nick," Lerch said. "You're the only expert on stogies on the premises."

"The ash closest to Rupert is from his cigar. It's a Montecristo Churchill from the Dominican Republic. I sold Stan six boxes of that brand this morning. Two of them are on that shelf next to a stack of videotapes and the photocopying machine. He left four in his locker in my humidor room. One of these boxes has been opened. May I lift the lid?" He glanced at Evert. "I'm sure the only fingerprints on the box will be Rupert's, mine, and possibly those of one of my employees who picked up the shipment of these Montecristos at Logan Airport on Saturday."

"Go ahead," said Lerch. "Open the box."

"Two cigars have been removed. The Montecristo Churchill is seven inches long. Match the ash with the end of the butt in the tray and you'll find they are the same diameter. We in the cigar business call the thickness of a cigar ring gauge. By the way, the ashes indicate this was not a hurried killing. So that would rule out this being a robbery."

"How do you figure that?" asked Evert.

"Stan had smoked almost half of his Churchill. That'd take about twenty minutes. The length of both the ashes are about the same. That puts Stan sitting across this desk from the other man talking with him, each smoking a Montecristo Churchill for at the very least twenty minutes. That's when Rupert laid his cigar in the ashtray, the butt pointed in his direction, and stood up. The killer set his cigar down, too, leaving the same length ash in the tray, got up, went behind Rupert, and did the deed. The body dropped sideways, landing where it is."

"So Rupert must have trusted him."

"Enough to give him a cigar and chat for twenty minutes."

"Hold it. You theorize that before he cut Rupert's throat the killer also put down his cigar—"

"He had to. He needed both hands."

"How do you know the cigar in the ashtray was Rupert's?"

"As long as I've known him he was an offie."

Lerch looked at him blankly. "Beg pardon?"

"An offie is someone who removes the band before he smokes. Since there's only one band in the ashtray, whoever was with Stan did not remove the one on his cigar."

Lerch smiled mischievously. "Maybe he collects cigar bands."

"A Montecristo Churchill is an excellent cigar, but the brand is too plentiful for their bands to be collectible. Unless it's a Montecristo made in Cuba, which these Montecristos aren't. That's why I say that the man who spent some time smoking with Rupert customarily leaves the band on. You might want to keep the contents of the ashtray out of news reports."

"Why a *man*? Lots of women are smoking cigars these days."

"A throat slit from behind is a masculine thing. You need strength to jerk the victim's head back and hold it as you cut the throat with the other, especially if the victim's standing."

"Two killers?" asked Evert. "One to immobilize and one to do the slicing?"

"I think if there'd been two killers, this would have been a stabbing. One grabs from behind and holds. The other stabs."

Lerch nodded. "If two cigars were smoked and there's only one butt, then the killer took his cigar with him so there'd be no chance of us tying it to him."

"I don't think you'd find fingerprints on a cigar butt," Nick said.

Lerch smiled. "I was talking about extracting his DNA from the saliva in the butt. Great things have happened in that area in the fifteen years since you retired, Nick.'' Turning to Evert, he said, ''I want Rupert's house secured.''

Nick interjected, ''It's a big green Victorian on Cowperthwaite Street. You can't miss it.''

''Then first thing in the morning,'' Lerch continued to Evert, ''I want you to take a squad and go over it with your fine-tooth comb.'' Turning to Nick, he asked, ''Can you come down to headquarters in the morning and give a detailed statement?''

''I'll type it up tonight. But I've been out of the statement business so long I'm not sure I remember how to write one.''

Lerch slapped Nick's back. ''Yeah. Right.''

## *Seven*

WAITING FOR A traffic light to change to permit pedestrians across Harvard Square, Nick chuckled at the irony of what had transpired. Almost twenty years ago a punk kid with a gun had gotten a drop on him, causing him to bow out of police work and take up the tobacco trade. Now, suddenly, all he had learned in fifteen years peddling smoke had turned him into a sleuth again!

In those few minutes spent making observations at the scene of a crime, he decided as he made the turn at Brattle Square and walked slowly in the direction of The Happy Smoking Ground, he'd done pretty well. He had succeeded in showing Jack Lerch that the motive for Stanley Rupert's life being taken in such a brutal way could not have been mere robbery.

This had been a killing so cunningly planned and carried out that the victim was caught off-guard and quietly executed. The perpetrator had walked away, no doubt blithely confident that he had committed a perfect murder.

While there was no such thing, there were plenty that were not solved. Whether this would be one of those now rested in the hands of Jack Lerch. And he was welcome to it!

With spotlights illuminating the green and gold sign on the facade of The Happy Smoking Ground and light emanating from the bay windows as he approached the store, he noted with relief but at the same time a pang of disappointment that during his absence the wooden Indian had gone unmolested by marauding pranksters of the current crop of Harvard Law School's first-year students.

Looking up at the light in the windows of Roger Woolley's third-floor apartment, he again heard the faint rattle of a typewriter, presumably banging out exploits of Woolley's dashingly handsome and brainy young detective for whom no homicide went unsolved. Deliciously tricky paperback novels, they unfolded in groves of academia bearing a strong resemblance to Harvard. Published under a pen name that was Roger Woolley's mischievous adoption of the names of two authors of the first two New Testament gospels, the plots followed a formula whose red herrings planted to mislead readers never diverted Inspector Jake Elwell from unmasking the murderer in the final chapter, ideally in the very last line.

How it came about that a professor of medieval history took up writing mystery novels was a puzzle Roger Woolley had never explained satisfactorily. If he were in a joking mood he said, "I made up my mind to prove that crime *does* pay. Unfortunately, I've discovered that it does not pay *enough*." On another occasion he'd waxed philosophical: "I am enchanted by the moral symmetry found only in the murder-mystery genre, namely, that goodness not only always triumphs over evil, but *must*. This is astonishing in a world whose bloody history attests that organized religion has yet to demonstrate to anyone that it promotes that concept beyond platitudinizing it from pulpits."

Deciding not to inform Woolley that a real murder had been committed that night and that the victim was his friend, but to knock on the professor's door first thing in the morning, Nick unlocked a door leading to a stairway that ascended to the apartments above the store, gathered mail addressed to Woolley from the floor beneath the mail slot, and wearily climbed the steps.

Opening the door to his own apartment on the second floor, he switched on a ceiling light. A small living room whose walls conveyed the pounding of the upstairs type-

writer was a mixture of furnishings, useful and merely dec-
orative accessories, and other acquistions from which any
detective worth his salary would deduce that the person
living within its walls did not mind if a stranger found out
everything about him. Titles in a tall corner bookcase revealed a man whose reading had been primarily related to
work as a cop.

Scrapbooks on a shelf held clippings of his cases that
made newspaper headlines.

A large assortment of other police-related objects ranged
from a plaster figurine of a fat cop in the uniform and
beehive helmet of the New York Police Department when
Theodore Roosevelt had been police commissioner, to an
astonishing array of images in porcelain and pewter of the
bane of existence of many generations of Scotland Yard
detectives, Sherlock Holmes.

Evidence that Nick Chase had been the adoring husband
of a sweet Irish gal named Maggie, proud father of a handsome son by the name of Kevin and a daughter called Jean,
as beautiful as she was headstrong, was found in pictures
of them adorning walls and tables. Scattered throughout the
room were objects collected during family vacations—souvenir knick-knacks and gimcracks from here and there.
Most of them had been bought by him.

A curious fact concerning his cluttered living room was
that the first time women looked at its accumulation of
things, they invariably asked, "Who dusts?"

His pat answer was, "Nobody. It's a proven fact that
after a while dust doesn't get any deeper." The serious
reply—the one he had given to Peg Baron—was "Happy
memories should be kept where you can see them."

Interestingly, and probably instructively, no male had
ever raised the issue of who did the housecleaning.

Regarding things someone did not want known, as every
cop had learned on the job or grasped instinctively in the
surprisingly brief history of organized policing—little more
than a century and a half—one had to peek into closets and
drawers of the bedroom.

A small space without a window at the rear of the apartment, his sleeping space—barely larger than a jail cell—

contained the double bed he had shared with Maggie in conceiving their children, a nightstand topped with a lamp, clock radio, and telephone, and a bureau with attached mirror that clumsy movers had managed to inflict with a small crack in the lower left corner.

Indeed, the only recently acquired object in the bedroom stood on a dangerously rickety card table. A computer with printer was a gift from conspiring offspring. Daughter Jean had envisioned the thing as a weapon in furtherance of her unrelenting campaign to turn him into a memoirist. Kevin had chipped in because he saw the device as potentially useful in tracking the fluctuating inventory of the store below. And playing video games.

While appreciative of his children's generosity, he'd found each one's motivations in wanting him to have and use a computer contradictory to each one's nature. Kevin had grown up to be a wordsmith in his career as a reporter for the *Globe*, as well as adjunct teacher of journalism at Boston University, so he should have been the one pushing him to write an autobiography. Instead the pressure came from the daughter who had chosen to follow him into fighting crime, although not by carrying a weapon, but as a criminalist for the Boston Police Department.

Had the murder of Stanley Rupert occurred across the river, he mused as he sat at the wobbly card table, *both* his children could have been expected to show up at the crime scene. For Kevin the goal would have been learning who, what, where, and when. Jean would have collected anything at the crime scene that might give her the how and the why.

A flick of thumb turned on the computer.

Advice concerning exactly which of the myriad apparatuses available on the market could best accomplish Jean and Kevin's different purposes had been provided by young Craig Spencer. A part-time employee of The Happy Smoking Ground, he also had insisted on installing a security system that included concealment of a tiny television camera lens in the frame displaying Nick's police shield, with a recording device capable of taping for twenty-four hours hidden in the humidor box on a shelf below.

"You really ought to have a setup like this in front of

the store, too,'' he had argued. ''It might put an end to annual thefts of your wooden Indian.''

That idea had been dismissed with ''And spoil a tradition?''

Further interest in surveillance cameras was soon eclipsed by a Spencer plan to use a computer to explore expanding the sale of tobacco and various equipment for consuming it via a worldwide network of computer users. Although he envisioned creation of a kind of electronic mail-order catalog known as a Web page with the same name as the store, the merchandising plan had yet to materialize, or, as Craig termed it, ''get up and running.''

The descriptive phrases applied to Spencer by Roger Woolley were ''techno-freak'' and ''computer nerd.'' But Craig had succeeded in showing Nick how to operate a computer as a fancy typewriter, the chief virtue of which was fixing the inescapable mistakes of the hunt-and-peck system of typing used by most cops of Nick's generation. With the computer there was no more making it all the way to the end of a page, hitting the wrong key—or discovering incorrect spelling or grammar—ripping the paper from the roller, and having to start over. During years of typing crime reports he had to have gone through reams of report forms. But now he could spot an error on the screen, fix it, and have the computer print out a flawless page. And for writing very late at night, it was quieter than Woolley's clanking typewriter, although he did miss hearing the bell when he came to the end of a line.

Rather than the clickety-clickety-click-bing, the tips of two rapidly moving fingers writing the statement requested by Jack Lerch produced tap-uh-tap-uh-tap-uhs and the end of the line took care of itself.

In black letters against the white background of the glowing screen he again explained how it had happened that he had been the first to discover the body. Regarding Rupert's transparent ploy to get him there, he could offer no explanation.

Like most homicides, it had been an intimate act. A murder between a couple of friends, or at least acquaintances. The two cigars proved it. Nobody gave a fine cigar to an enemy. Sharing good cigars was a bond. A civilized act. When Stan Rupert opened his new box of Montecristo Churchills and handed one to the man seated at the opposite side of the desk, he did so in friendship. Or so he'd thought.

The killing had been premeditated, of course. Whoever had ventured into that cluttered back room had done so with murder in mind. This was not death delivered on the spur of the moment.

The weapon itself provided evidence of stealthy murder. A knife was more certain of inflicting death than a pistol. And equally important to killing someone and getting away from the scene, a knife blade slicing a throat was not likely to attract anyone else's attention.

Approaching Rupert's store, he had seen no one leaving it. Pausing a moment to ponder timing, he wondered if he had not slowed his pace and not stopped to look in the windows of Leavitt & Peirce and the bookstore and instead knocked on Stan Rupert's door ten minutes sooner, might Stanley still be alive?

Judging the condition of the blood as he observed it from the doorway to the back room, Rupert's throat had to have been slit not much before eight-fifteen. Had he appeared outside the store at eight-ten, Nick wondered as he hit the Save button and then Print, might he have seen Stan's killer leave the store? Recognized him?

Reading the errorless three-page statement that had been ejected by the printer, he wondered if the murderer had ever set foot in The Happy Smoking Ground.

# Eight

WHEN THE PHONE woke him, the ingrained habit of the homicide detective dictated turning toward the glowing face of the bedside clock to note the time. Hands pointed to 11:10. Darkness outside the small window told him it was P.M.

The agitated voice responding to his sleepy hello was his son's. "Dad, what's this about you discovering a murder victim?"

Nick sat up in bed. "Which hat have you got on, Kevin? Is it your newspaperman's fedora?"

"Yes. I'm calling a witness to the crime of murder."

"To be accurate, I was a witness at the *scene* of a murder. I was not there when it happened." Turning on the bedside light, he looked across the room to the card table where he had left his statement in an envelope. "What did the police tell you?"

"All Jack Lerch would say was that it was you who found Stanley Rupert's body."

"So what more is there to know?"

"Dad, what in blazes were you *doing* there?"

"I can't see how that could possibly be of any interest to the readers of the *Globe*."

"Well it's of considerable interest to me."

"Ah! You've switched hats. We're now off the record?"

"Yes, we are."

"I went there on a business matter."

"At eight in the evening?"

"You know I don't close my store till eight on Mondays."

"Has it dawned on you, Dad, that you could have walked in on that murder in progress?"

"Of course it has. Too bad I didn't."

"You might have ended up being killed."

"Possible. But highly unlikely."

"I see. You would have cold-cocked the killer and held him till the cops came."

"Something like that. Has your sister heard about this?"

"I haven't spoken to Jean. I've been working the story and just got back to the paper. She could have heard on the news."

"If she had she would have called me by now."

"I remember now. Jeanie told me she and Mike Tinney were going to a BSO concert."

"Ah, yes. The Tchaikovsky first piano concerto! I had the offer of a ticket from Peg Baron. But I had another engagement."

"At a murder scene."

"Not a new experience for me, Kev."

"That's true, but it's been a lot of years since murder was your line of work. How well did you know Stanley Rupert?"

"You're asking this wearing which of your hats?"

"The newspaperman's."

"How well I knew Stan Rupert is no business of the press."

"Obviously you knew him well enough to call him Stan."

"That's very, very good, Kev! He was a valued customer of long standing. I've known Stan since I set up shop on Brattle Street. He was quite a genial fellow."

Kevin grunted. "That's not what his neighbors told me. They said he was as nasty a piece of work as you could find."

"He wasn't when he bought cigars from me."

"What can you tell me of the murder scene as you found it?"

With another glance at the envelope addressed to Lerch, Nick said, "I could tell you a lot. But I'm not going to. And if you put that quote in your story it won't matter that you're thirty-five years old. I will tan your backside."

"I'm not going to quote you, dad. And I'm thirty-seven."

"How are Noreen and the kids?"

"I'm off tomorrow. Come to dinner and see for yourself."

"I will. Now suppose you get back to work so this retired copper can get back to sleep."

"All right, Dad. G'night."

Picking up the ringing phone again almost immediately and expecting the equally alarmed voice of his daughter, he answered jovially, "So how was the concert, darling?"

"Never mind that, you old fart," demanded Peg Baron. "What I want to know is are you okay?"

"Other than being kept from getting my beauty sleep, I have never felt better, thank you."

"Nicholas Chase, you are without doubt the most maddening individual I have ever known!"

"Including twenty-something cigar-smoking piano virtuosos?"

"Are you aware you are all over the news on radio and TV?"

"I went to bed early. Not that it's done me any good. All I've done is answer the phone."

"You found a man horribly murdered! How could you possibly expect to sleep?"

"Yeah. I should have left my phone off the hook."

Uttering a throaty growl, she hung up.

Ten minutes later Jean was cool, calm, and the consummate criminalist. Without preliminaries she said, "I understand your observations of the murder scene were pretty amazing."

"A handful of trifles!"

"I heard it was an ashtray."

"Who told you about that?"

"When I heard your name on the news just a few minutes ago I called Jack Lerch for confirmation. He was mighty impressed by your performance at the crime scene.''

''Jack's too generous. But I'm glad to hear he thinks what I had to say might be helpful in cracking what's going to be a very difficult case to close.'' He gazed at the envelope on the card table. ''Cracking it may be impossible.''

''Jack Lerch's homicide squad is awfully good.'' She paused a moment. ''This has to have been an awful experience for you, Dad. I assume that unfortunate man was a good friend.''

''Stan Rupert was more good customer than good friend. He was in my store early in the morning to pick up part of an order for six boxes of his favorite Montecristo Churchills. He left four in his locker and took two with him.''

''The ones you pointed out at the crime scene.''

With a smile in his voice, he said, ''You obviously got more out of Lerch than your brother did.''

''Oh good. You've talked to Kevin.''

''He was on the horn a few minutes ago, fishing for news.''

''In vain, I presume.''

''He removed his fisherman's chapeau long enough to ask how his old man was doing.''

She paused again. ''How *are* you doing, Dad?''

''I'm fine. The hardest part of this is going to be breaking the news of Rupert's murder to Roger Woolley. They *were* friends.''

''Not the first time you've been the harbinger of bad news.''

''Kevin told me you and Mike Tinney went to the symphony. How was the concert?''

''Has a performance of the Boston Symphony Orchestra ever not been great?''

''When are you finally going to make an honest man of Mike by marrying him?''

''That's what he's always asking me.''

''So what's the problem?''

After her longest pause of all, she sighed. ''It's still too soon to even consider taking that step.''

''Nonsense. Your divorce was four years ago.''

"Five and a half. Six months after Trish was born."

"That's a long time to keep a man waiting."

"Mike is very patient. For a cop."

"I happen to be talking about me. I need another grand-child to spoil. Your brother's one up on you!"

"I'm going to hang up now, Dad. Good night."

Ten minutes later the caller was Peg Baron again. "Cripes, Nick! Now I can't sleep. Apparently I can't leave you on your own one night! Are you sure you're okay?"

"Why shouldn't I be?"

"I don't know. I've never found the body of somebody who was robbed and murdered."

"Just between you, me, and the police, it wasn't robbery. It was cold-blooded premeditated murder. How was the Tchaikovsky? May I presume the kid got through it without flubbing a note?"

"Maestro Wieder performed brilliantly."

"Of course he did. Good cigars have that effect."

## Nine

ROGER WOOLLEY'S DREAM of chivalrous knights of King Arthur's Camelot had been delightful. He especially enjoyed the jousting between the evil and ambitious Mordred and the dashingly handsome and gallant Sir Galahad that resulted in the Lady of the Lake and Queen Guinevere paying up for foolishly wagering a professor of medieval history that Mordred would unhorse Galahad. And there was the appearance of Morgan le Fay in jogging suit and sneakers using the sword Excalibur like a baton to conduct the Boston Pops in "Stars and Stripes Forever" at the Fourth of July concert on the Charles River Esplanade. But now, to his dismay, stimulating debate in Harvard Yard with Jerome Lazarus in the role of Merlin on the virtues of meerschaum pipes vis-à-vis those made of briarwood was being interrupted by a loud banging on the Widener Library doors. Mystifyingly imitating the voice of Nick Chase, Inspector Jake Elwell was demanding, "Open up, Professor."

Only half awake, Woolley stared blankly at the wall next to the bed and wondered what had possessed Jake Elwell to search for Slattery in the Widener Library. Everyone knew that the prime suspect in the murder of Colonel Yancy had driven Amelia and her friend Floyd up to Rockport so Amelia could paint yet another of her adequate but tedious watercolor renderings of Motif No. 1.

The door banging persisted.

"Roger! Are you in there?"

Suddenly wide awake, Woolley bolted up. "Who's there?"

"It's Nick Chase."

Woolley sniffed the air. "Are we on fire?"

"No! But I do have some bad news."

"Hold your horses," Woolley answered, throwing back a tangle of sheets and groping the foot of the bed for a threadbare purple robe. Opening the door, he surveyed Nick's drawn expession. "Dear boy, you look absolutely awful."

"I'm sorry to get you up so early—"

Woolley yawned. "What time is it?"

"Six o'clock. I wanted to tell you before you could hear it on the news or read about it in the paper."

Woolley stepped back and opened the door wide. "Do come in."

While the apartment was laid out like the one below, everything else about it contrasted dramatically with Nick's ex-cop life. This was a home furnished by a scholar of an era long past whose literature took notice only of murders of kings, queens, princes, pretenders to power, and conquerors.

In a corner of the living room atop a sturdy table next to Woolley's exercise equipment stood an aged upright Underwood typewriter. Beside it lay a tape recorder and half-finished manuscript providing mute testimony that the lively septuagenarian occupant of the third-floor apartment above The Happy Smoking Ground had educated himself equally well in means, methods, and motives of modern murder. Prolific evidence of this took up an entire shelf of a bookcase in the form of Inspector Jake Elwell novels and their reprints in a dozen languages.

Unsure how to begin, Nick handed Woolley his mail.

"Ah, a long-awaited and much-needed royalty check," said Woolley. But a delightful smile quickly changed to a frown. "I know that look of yours. Something is amiss. No point in hemming and hawing, Nick. I'm a grown-up. Let me have the bad news."

Nick took a deep breath, then exhaled, "There's been a tragic death."

Woolley gasped. "Not in your delightful family I hope!"

"Thank God, no."

"Then it has to be another in the rapidly dwindling phalanx of which I spoke yesterday in your store. Which of my colleagues has at last journeyed into that undiscovered country from whose bourn no traveler returns? Jerome Lazarus?"

"Stanley Rupert," said Nick, sitting in the corner of a sagging sofa. "He was murdered."

Woolley leaned forward. "When? Where? By whom?"

"Last night in the office at the rear his store. We don't know who did it. Or why. I'm sure it wasn't a robbery. The method was all wrong."

The mystery writer asked, "How was he killed?"

"His throat was cut."

The professor sank back in the chair. "How ghastly!"

"Judging by all I observed at the scene—"

"You were there? But of course you were! Because of that ruse Stanley invented to lure you there last evening!"

"It happened only a few minutes before I arrived," Nick said as he pushed up from the sofa. "It appears that Stan had to have known his killer."

Woolley also rose. "*Appears* that he knew him? Of course he knew him. Unfortunately, Stanley evidently didn't pick up on the hatred that must have been seething secretly for who knows how long."

"Why do you say secretly?"

"If someone hates you enough to wish to cut your throat, and makes no secret of it, you are more than likely to pick up on it. You would hardly leave yourself as vulnerable as Stan made the mistake of doing last night. When you investigate this case, you are going to find Stanley's murderer among his intimate circle."

"Careful what you say, Roger," Nick said, chuckling as he drifted toward the door. "Jack Lerch may consider you a suspect."

"He's investigating this?"

"But you couldn't have murdered Rupert. When I came

back from the scene of the crime the lights were on in your windows and you were beating the devil out of your typewriter.''

"Inspector Elwell was finally getting off his duff. The man is positively maddening at times. He can be a study in inertia." Slapping a hand to his chest, Woolley exclaimed, "Oh good grief. I suppose it's going to fall on me to arrange a proper sendoff for poor old Stanley."

"He had no relatives?"

"Oh, he had them. There was a wife he walked out on a long time ago, leaving her with a young daughter. Now there are also a grandson and a nephew. They are in their twenties. There's no one around to notify them of Stan's death but me."

"The police department may be able to help you with that. Get in touch with Lerch."

"I hope you offered to lend Jack the Nimble your assistance in finding Stan's murderer."

"Don't be ridiculous. I haven't worked a homicide in almost twenty years."

"So what?"

"I've gone as stale as a five-cent cigar."

"Balderdash! Once a homicide detective, always a homicide detective. Crime solving is like riding a bicycle. You can never forget how."

"Is that one of Jake Elwell's sayings?"

Woolley winked. "It soon will be."

"This isn't one of those murders in a mystery novel in which an outsider steps in to save the bacon of the official police. I have every confidence that Jack Lerch will solve Stanley Rupert's murder without me."

"Lerch would be a fool not to bring you in as his partner."

"He's already *got* a partner."

"You refer to Sergeant Gary Evert?"

Nick opened the door. "I believe that's his name."

"That man is not a detective," exclaimed Woolley as Nick started down the stairs. "He's a damn fool. He's such a dolt that he has failed to discern that in my Jake Elwell books the stupid bumbling Sergeant Les Street is based on *him*.''

"I must say," Nick said, pausing on the stairs, "you seem to be taking this news about your friend Stan pretty well.''

"In the words of the seventeenth-century metaphysical poet George Herbert:

> *And now in age I bud again,*
> *After so many deaths I live and write.*''

Two hours later, with walking stick swinging from his right hand and his new pipe clenched between his teeth as he passed the bay window of The Happy Smoking Ground, Woolley offered a wave to Nick and continued on. Reaching Harvard Square and negotiating a path through a rush of pedestrians, he felt haunted by a vivid memory of Sunday's sickly expression on Stanley's Rupert's face. But as he passed through a gateway between Lehman Hall and Wadsworth House into Harvard Yard, he recalled it was this same route taken by Jake Elwell toward a fateful rendezvous with Reggie Hawkings in *The Deadly Dons*. Ahead and to the left was the office of the university police, and off to the right the Widener Library, site of Sunday morning's encounter between Rupert and Lazarus.

Dwarfing all its surroundings since its completion in 1914 and named for Harry Elkins Widener, who in 1912 went down with the *Titanic*, the library building had provided the setting for murder in the first Jake Elwell novel to have been reviewed in the book section of the Sunday *Globe*.

"This second outing of pseudonymous author Matthew Mark's sleuth holds out the delightful prospect," said the critic, "that Harvard is headed for a reputation as a homicidal campus equal to Oxford University in the Inspector Morse novels of Colin Dexter.''

But why not? Was there a literary rule requiring stuffiness, intellectual cliques, scholarly snobs, condescendingly cloistered minds, raw ambition, rampant jealousy, backbiting, backstabbing, and the occasional murder be reserved

for the academic bastions of Britain? In other words, why
should they have all the fun? There could be found within
the encompassing red brick walls of Harvard Yard, in cor-
ridors and rooms of venerable halls beyond the Yard, and
in the ultramodern architecture of the John F. Kennedy
School of Government, the residences of Dunster House
and Leverett House Towers, and other edifices every bit as
much motivation to murder as Inspector Morse and real-
life British police encountered in places that had been familiar to Sir Walter Raleigh of tobbaco fame, Matthew
Arnold, Thomas Hobbes, Horace Walpole, Christopher
Marlowe, Rupert Brooke, Lord Chesterfield, and Bill Clin-
ton. Even a dissident preacher who'd emigrated from England and bequeathed his private library to a college
founded in 1636, in the heart of which now stood his
statue—John Harvard.

Oblivious to students and the occasional professor on
their way to classes, he came to University Hall, the architect Charles Bulfinch's masterpiece of gray Chelmsford
granite, white wooden pilasters, and graceful chimneys.
Passing Daniel Chester French's statue of the college's patron in front, he entered the hall and slowly ascended to
the second floor on the granite staircase made from blocks
of stone that seemed to hang unsupported.

Expecting to find Lazarus adhering to his ritual of reading newspapers in the Faculty Room before convening his
nine o'clock seminar, he was perplexed. Assuming he must
have missed him by minutes, he returned to the ground
floor and hurried to a small chamber long ago claimed by
Lazarus as both an office and the ideal place of edification
for students at work on senior theses in recent European
history. A note tacked to the door read:

Seminars and Student conferences are canceled.

                                                    J.L.

This probably would be welcome by the students concerned, Woolley thought as he turned away, but it was a

very unusual thing for Jerome Lazarus to do. Perhaps unprecedented.

Outside again, he paused for a moment by the John Harvard statue. Peering toward Appleton Chapel, he supposed it would be the appropriate place for a gathering of persons who might care to reflect on the life of Stanley Rupert. Walking on, he allowed the possibility that someone might even mourn him.

Hoping to find Lazarus in the chummy confines of the nearby Faculty Club, he peeked into each of its sitting rooms and found among a few familiar figures and more that there was no one who recalled seeing Jerome Lazarus that morning.

Outside, chewing the bit of his new briar pipe, he startled a pretty raven-haired coed with, ''This is *very* worrying indeed.''

## Ten

"HOLY HOMICIDE, NICK," exclaimed Sam Gargan as he exploded through the door at ten o'clock. "Did you really find that guy who was murdered the way the news on the radio says you did?"

"If the news on the radio said I found a man murdered," Nick said around the day's second Upmann, "the answer is yes."

With skinny arms extending from the short white sleeves of an MIT T-shirt, knobby elbows resting on the wood top of the display case, and slender torso slanted forward eagerly, Sam said, "Man, that's so cool. It's like something from one of Woolley's detective yarns. Do the cops know who did it?"

"If they'd made an arrest it would have been on the news."

"Will they?"

"I expect so."

"Are you gonna give 'em the benefit of your expertise?"

"The only thing I'm giving the police is a formal statement. And while I'm delivering it to police headquarters you'll have to watch the store. I trust your seminar went okay last night."

Sam's lanky posture sagged into a slump. "Not exactly."

Plucking the cigar from his mouth, Nick glowered. "Oh? What happened?"

"Her name," said Sam as black eyebrows arched as though they belonged to Groucho Marx, "was Brenda."

"Romancing women," Nick scolded as he came out from behind the counter, "is not going to result in your getting a degree in electrical engineering."

"You know what, boss?" Sam said, running a hand over his brush-cut hair. "Sometimes you can be a real spoilsport."

"I hope you're not seeing Wanda tonight. I need you to keep an eye on the store. My son's invited me to dinner."

"*Bon appétit.* And her name is Brenda."

Bisecting Cambridge for much of its length between Harvard in the center of the city and the MIT campus on the western side of the Charles River and running in a nearly straight line, Massachusetts Avenue offered echoes of the city's history as a place known not only for citadels of intellectual pursuits, but for bastions of industry and commerce. While John Harvard had come from England and endowed a college, down from a poor farm in New Hampshire had come a lad whose ability to make soap had resulted in Lever Brothers. And a sixteen-year-old ship's cook who learned how to make coffins became founder of the National Casket Company. As Harvard flourished in the 1800s, eight times as many workers as the college had students engaged in manufacturing soap, ladders, carriages, piano keys, flowerpots, hats, the first mechanical eggbeater, ink, paper cartons, rubber, valves, reversible collars, boilers, bread, crackers, and candy as evidenced by the big gray plant about halfway between Harvard and MIT making quarter-size rolls of Necco Wafers.

Barely a mile from The Happy Smoking Ground, Nick passed City Hall on his left, turned right off Massacusetts to Pleasant Street and left again on Green. Considering himself lucky to find a space for his car, he parked almost directly in front of police department headquarters. Although it was a dwarf compared to the immense square pile of red brick he remembered as New York City's One Police

Plaza, the small, gray stone building evoked a sense of comfortable familiarity.

Discovering Lerch's third-floor office open, he looked in to find the detective unshaven and coatless with the sleeves of his white shirt rolled up to his elbows. Behind a desk littered with papers he appeared even more rumpled than he had the previous night.

Two knocks on the door caused him to look up. "Hello, Nick! I didn't expect to see you here so soon."

"If you're tied up I can come back later."

"Hell no. Come in. Pull up a chair. Has daylight given you any new insights into this confounding case?"

Nick placed the envelope containing his statement on the desk. "Everything I know is in here. There's nothing different from last night."

Lerch reared back in the tiltable chair. "Your version of Sherlock Holmes impressed the hell out of Sergeant Evert."

"I was equally impressionable when I was his age. But I find it harder and harder to believe I was ever that young."

"I know how you feel. For me the years show in the legs."

"Of course, I could be miles off base about this not having been a robbery."

"If you are wrong we're dealing with the stupidest thief in history," said Lerch, coming upright in his chair. "After you left and everything in that office was dusted for fingerprints, Evert and I were able to give the place a thorough going over. In the middle drawer of the desk we discovered hundred-dollar bills in packs of ten. There were fifteen of 'em."

Nick let out a long low whistle. "Fifteen grand?"

"*With* the wrappers still around 'em."

Nick thought a moment. "New notes or used?"

Lerch grinned. "They've all been in circulation."

"Rupert could have made a big sale that day."

"Possibly. But I've been thinking about what you said last night about people who buy things from Rupert paying by check or credit card. So I've dispatched Evert to check the banks all over Cambridge, and if needs be in Boston, to see if there's a record of anybody withdrawing fifteen grand. Federal law requires banks and other financial institutions to report cash transactions of more than ten grand. It's part of the feds' so-called drug war. Since that law's been in effect, drug dealers have come up with some imaginative ways to launder their ill-gotten gains.''

''I find it hard to believe that Rupert's antiques business was a front for drug peddlers. He could have made a big sale.''

''I've also got my people checking that. Assuming, of course, that Rupert wasn't dodging the tax man by keeping some sales off the books.''

Nick made a clucking sound. ''What suspicious minds you detectives have!''

''But all that is beside the point you made last night, that this murder wasn't the result of a robbery gone wrong. Finding all that money bears that out. Having killed Rupert, the perpetrator wouldn't have left without looking for something to make murder worthwhile. That leaves the inescapable conclusion that he went there to kill Rupert. The trouble is, the only clue he left behind was that cigar ash. You know the rule concerning timing in a homicide investigation.''

Nick nodded. ''If you can't solve a murder case in forty-eight hours, odds are you aren't going to solve it. I'm sure you will, Jack. It's still early in the game.''

''The press is not so patient. I've had a slew of calls this morning, including two from your son.''

''And one from my daughter last night.''

''That was out of concern for her old man.''

''The really infuriating thing about having grown children,'' Nick said, rising to leave, ''is that they have a difficult time understanding how their parents managed to make it so far through life without their assistance.''

''Mercifully my three haven't reached that age yet,'' Lerch said, accompanying him to the door. ''What can you tell me about Rupert's family?''

''I knew him only as a customer.''

"For how long?"

"Since I opened my store. That's almost fifteen years. But the man was over seventy years old. Who can say how many enemies he could have made in all that time? For all the data on Rupert's family I suggest you talk to Roger Woolley."

Lerch's face went pale. "Oh hell. Not that damn scribbler of mystery yarns in which the police have yet to solve a case on their own! What's Woolley got to do with Rupert?"

"Roger and Stanley became friends in the Second World War, then met again as undergrads at Harvard, and were faculty colleagues after that. Shall I ask him to give you a call?"

"I prefer to drop in on him."

Having failed to reach Lazarus by telephone and thinking the worst, Woolley had hurried from the Harvard campus to the Chapman Arms Apartments on University Road. It had been here in chapter eight of *Death Penalty* that Jake Elwell in his desperate search for Jim Trainer had jimmied the door of an apartment whose description was a duplicate of Lazarus's four-room digs.

Feigning outrage to mask his delight, Lazarus had protested, "How dare you invade my privacy in this way?"

"I see no point in going to all the trouble of dreaming up places when I can use ones that already exist."

Now, ten years after the novel's publication, the ringing of the doorbell of Lazarus's apartment proved unavailing. Finding a coveralls-clad Chapman Arms janitor, he urgently demanded, "Have you seen Professor Lazarus this morning?"

Looking up from mopping the floor of the lobby, the sullen youth with the build of a Boston Celtics basketball player rubbed a scruffy three-day beard and answered gruffly, "He went away."

Woolley gripped both of the youth's iron biceps. "When?"

Broad shoulders shrugged off Woolley's grasp. "He was

just goin' out the door when I was comin' on shift at five-thirty. ''

''Did he mention when he'd be back?''

''Nope. But it'll be a couple of days at least.''

''Why do you say that?''

''I helped him lug a couple of suitcases out to his car.''

''Nonsense. Professor Lazarus doesn't own a car.''

''This was a hired one.''

''But he doesn't drive. He doesn't even have a license.''

''It wasn't a *rental*,'' the basketball player grumbled. ''This was a limousine. The kind rich people hire to take them out to Logan Airport.''

## Eleven

"POPPYCOCK," MUTTERED WOOLLEY contemptuously a few moments later as he followed the easy curve of University Road toward a dead end at Mount Auburn Street. While Lazarus was by no means a poor man struggling to get by on Social Security checks and a meager pension, he was never a free spender. If he had shelled out the cost of limousine service to the airport, he had not done so out of a sense of urgency. He had hired a limo because he felt he had to. But what could have motivated a retired old historian to step out of character and into an airport limousine at five-thirty in the morning?

Reaching Mount Auburn Street, he recalled the last time he'd seen Lazarus. Sunday morning in the Widener. Rushing like a madman toward Rupert. "Stanley!" he'd shouted, gaunt face, scarecrow arms flailing. "It's urgent I speak to you."

Crossing Mount Auburn Street, he wondered why Rupert had told Lazarus to come to his shop at four o'clock. Why hadn't he let Lazarus explain himself then and there?

Walking on, he reached Story Street. But before turning to the right, there came to him one of those flashes of illumination and understanding that happened so readily to Jake Elwell, yet were always so hard for Matthew Mark to put into words on paper.

After pondering this a moment he cried, "Of course!"

That was the only logical explanation, he thought. Exultantly tapping the paving with the tip of his walking stick, he increased his pace to Brattle Street. When he reached The Happy Smoking Ground he found the proprietor was not in.

"Buying a pipe as a gift for your boyfriend is a very nice gesture," Sam Gargan was saying to an attractive young woman as Woolley entered the store, "but it can also be a tricky thing. Even a risky one."

The woman gazed at him, mystified.

"You see, a pipe is as personal a choice as buying a suit of clothes or a pair of shoes. Or a necktie! Like all those things, a pipe involves how a man sees himself in terms of his status in life. And how he wants others to see him. It's an ego thing. And it's a matter of vanity. A pipe should match a man's style, his personality. And even the shape of his head. The cut of his jaw."

Still perplexed, the young woman asked, "Are you saying I shouldn't buy him a pipe?"

"I'm saying that the only way to know if you're making the right selection," said Gargan with a glance at Woolley, "is to have him with you when you purchase it, so he can try it on as he would a suit, a tie, or pair of shoes."

"But it's the present I was planning to give him at a surprise birthday party tonight."

Gargan smiled. "We do have gift certificates."

She made a disapproving face. "I hate giving people those things. They're so impersonal, if you know what I mean. What is your return policy? May I choose a pipe, and if he doesn't like it he can bring it back and select another?"

"That is certainly an option. However, since it's a gift from you, he probably won't want to hurt your feelings by exchanging it for another. Of course, he could wind up stuck with a pipe he's not in love with."

The young woman giggled. "You've got to be kidding me. How can anyone love a pipe?"

"I've known of men who loved certain pipes so much

they left instructions that they wanted to be buried with them.''

Fascinated by the conversation, but with growing impatience, Woolley strode toward the rear of the store. As he approached, he recited:

> *"There may be comrades in this world,*
> *As stanch and true as steel.*
> *There are: and by their friendships firm*
> *Is life made only real.*
> *But after all, of all these hearts*
> *That close to mine entwine,*
> *None lie so near, nor seem so dear*
> *As this old pipe of mine."*

The young woman pressed a delicate hand to her chest. "How very charming, sir."

"Excuse me for intruding, young lady," Woolley said, "but may I offer a suggestion?"

"Why of course!"

"Do you know your friend's brand of pipe tobacco?"

"As a matter of fact, I do," she said cheerily. "I don't usually care for the smell of tobacco smoke—"

"Most women don't."

"But I adore the kind he smokes in his pipes, so I asked him about it."

Gargan asked, "What was the name?"

"It's a Scottish brand."

Woolley asked, "McClelland, perhaps?"

"That's it!"

"May I propose that you purchase a pound can of McClelland *and* a gift certificate for a pipe?"

"That's a wonderful suggestion. Thank you very much."

Turning aside, Woolley said, "The pleasure was mine."

"Are you the owner of this store?"

"Alas, I am not," Woolley said as he turned round to Sam Gargan. "I'm surprised not to find him here this morning."

"He had something to take care of," said Gargan. "He went down to see someone . . . on Green Street."

"Yes, I can see why he would have business there. Did he say how long he'd be gone?"

"Afraid not, Professor."

"Please tell him as soon as he returns that I need to speak to him on a matter of grave urgency. I'll be upstairs."

Smoking his new pipe and awaiting Nick's return, Woolley sat before his typewriter staring at the blank sheet of paper that ought to contain the beginning of the fifth chapter in Inspector Elwell's investigation of the Constantine diamond robbery. Unless Jake got a move on, he would never discern the true motive for the murder of Eddie Richards that would lead him to the twist in the novel that would occur with breathtaking suddenness in the penultimate chapter.

However, instead of compelling Jake into action, he let his thoughts return to the question posed by the young woman concerning ownership of the store two floors below, and how it had happened that it had come to bear its felicitous name. Had he been able to garner an advance payment from a publisher for his first Inspector Elwell novel that his literary agent was able to demand for the one that awaited completion in his old typewriter, The Happy Smoking Ground might have been a bookstore with the name Fatal Attractions and purveying that highest form of intellectual stimulation—the mystery story.

As he puffed his pipe and stared at the unforgiving blank paper in his typewriter, further speculation upon the subject of what poet John Greenleaf Whittier had called the saddest words of all, "what might have been," ended with the ringing of the phone.

His gravelly "Hello" was answered by a deep baritone voice. "It's Nick Chase. What do you want to tell me that's so urgent?"

Except for an occasional puff of cigar smoke, Nick seemed as rooted in place as the wooden Indian outside as Woolley came to the conclusions to be drawn from his narrative. "Rupert would not, or could not, let Lazarus continue with whatever Lazarus had to say in the Widener on

Sunday because they were not alone. *I was there*. Now, two days later, one has been murdered and the other has packed a couple of suitcases, taken the unprecedented step of canceling his seminars, climbed into a hired limousine at five-thirty this morning, and gone *missing*.''

Stirring at last, Nick said, ''First of all, the janitor did not tell you Lazarus had gone missing. He said he went *away*.''

Glaring at Nick across the antique cash register, Woolley retorted, ''Lazarus has never before gone *away* without informing me as to his destination and when I should expect him back.''

''As the saying goes, there's always a first time.''

''Furthermore, he has always relied on me to drive him to the airport and to pick him up when he returned.''

''He probably didn't want to bother you.''

''What about the note canceling the seminars?''

''His students are probably delighted to have the time off.''

''In each instance when he did leave town he arranged for his seminars to be conducted by a substitute.''

Observing the long ash of his Upmann perilously close to dropping onto the cash register, Nick held the long cigar over a cupped palm and with a gentle tap let the ash fall into it. ''He probably didn't have time to look for a fill-in.''

''Nonsense. He could have turned to me. If he had time to leave the note on the door canceling his seminars, he had time to call me. Something's terribly wrong here, Nick. As sure as I'm standing here talking to you, the Rupert murder and Lazarus going missing are connected in some way.''

''Even for the creator of the Inspector Jake Elwell novels that's a big leap of imagination,'' Nick said, depositing the ash in a tray. ''But if you truly believe all this, you should talk to Jack Lerch, who, as it happens, desires to talk to you.''

Woolley's eyes narrowed to slits. ''Talk to me? About what?''

''He wants to know about Rupert's family and friends.''

"Other than myself and Lazarus, I know of no friends who are not deceased."

"Did Rupert have enemies?"

"Do you count students he flunked?"

"Have you considered the possibilty that Lazarus disappeared because *he* killed Rupert?"

"Don't be droll, Nick. Rupert's throat was cut by someone strong and sure of hand. Jerome Lazarus couldn't even shave himself using a blade. Arthritis in his fingers compelled him to switch to an electric razor years ago. I must say, Nick, for the man who found Rupert murdered, and a former homicide detective as well, you amaze me."

Nick plucked out the cigar. "Why is that?"

Woolley shrugged. "You seem unconcerned about what appears to me to be quite an unusual case with you in the middle."

"That's the mystery writer in you talking."

"What of the cop within you?"

"He's got the utmost confidence in Jack Lerch."

"How will you feel if Lerch fails?"

"Surprised."

Woolley smiled and stroked his beard. "You don't feel even the slightest nostalgia for your thrilling days of yesteryear?"

"The only thing I feel nostalgia for is the way my grandchildren squealed and hugged me when I came for dinner when they were little. Now they think they're too big for such things."

# Twelve

VIA THE MOST direct route to Tuesday dinner at the home of Kevin and Noreen Chase and their children, Nigel, age thirteen, and Celeste, age eleven, Nick could not escape reminders that The Happy Smoking Ground stood in the very heart of the territory of Harvard Unversity and one of its most revered graduates.

On his left as he drove down John F. Kennedy Street stood the John F. Kennedy School of Government. Crossing the Charles River, he passed between Harvard Stadium and the Harvard School of Business on Harvard Street. A long meandering thoroughfare, it cut through the tangled streets of the neighborhood of Allston to emerge on the south side of the long gash of the Massachusetts Turnpike and eventually reached the town of Brookline.

Founded in 1638 immediately west of Boston, Brookline was popularly known in the first decade of the twentieth century as the Town of Millionaires. But its chief claim to modern fame was found at No. 36 Beales Street. Roughly halfway between Commonwealth Avenue on the north and Beacon Street to the south, the U.S. government had carved out a National Historic Site that preserved for posterity the rather modest house of the latter-day millionaire Joseph P. Kennedy in which the thirty-fifth President of the United States had been born on May 29, 1917.

Crossing Beacon Street, Nick supposed that to grandchildren waiting to greet him on this cool spring evening, the history of John Kennedy must be as ancient as President Woodrow Wilson had seemed to him when he was Nigel's age. When JFK defeated Richard Nixon for President in 1960 the son who would be Nigel's father was in his mother's womb, with seven months to go before emerging into life. By the time his sister Jean was born, Lyndon Johnson presided over a country in which countless streets, buildings, arenas, stadiums, the space center of Cape Canaveral, Florida, and New York's Idlewild Airport had seen their names changed, perhaps too hastily, to Kennedy.

Finally turning off Harvard Street, he followed Longwood Road to a Tudor-style house. Bracketed by old trees with fresh leaves and looking bigger outside than it was within, it had been chosen by Kevin and Noreen because it stood across from Longwood Playground, a benefit for the kids, with public tennis courts for themselves. Parking his car behind two others in the driveway, he sniffed in the air the tantalizing aroma of Noreen's specialty, Irish lamb stew.

Ringing the doorbell, he braced himself for an onslaught of questions about Monday night in Rupert's antiques store, not only from his reporter-son and his wife, but from curious offspring.

Greeting him hugless and without squeals of delight, the two sandy-haired, blue-eyed children were replicas of their parents, except in height, although he expected Nigel would not be long in matching, and perhaps exceeding, Kevin's six feet one. That the boy might follow in his father's footsteps in choosing a career manifested itself immediately.

"Tell me all about the dead man you found, Granddad," Nigel exclaimed. "Was it a real bloody mess?"

Celeste's growing up to be as pert and pretty as both her mother and the grandmother she had not known was never in doubt. But her fleeting wince at her brother's question suggested that her becoming a journalist like her father was not in the cards.

The need to answer Nigel was prevented by the intercession of the male parent. "Granddad's been through enough without having to tell you the gruesome details. Dinner's ready. Wash your hands.''

Nigel pouted. ''I did that already.''

''Then go help your mother in the kitchen. Both of you!'' As they dutifully retreated, he added forcefully, ''And there will be no pestering Granddad at the table about what happened, either.''

''It's okay, Kev,'' said Nick as he watched the children go. ''I don't mind talking about it.''

With an impish smile as he made sure the children were gone, Kevin whispered, ''That's good, Dad, because Noreen and I intend to do our own pestering after we've driven the kids off to their rooms to do their homework.''

As Nick settled contentedly into a huge, deep, and softly encompassing club chair in the basement family room after dinner, and Kevin and Noreen sat close on a couch that had seen better days, Noreen announced, ''Gentlemen, you may smoke.''

''Thank you, my dear,'' said Nick, dipping a hand into the inside pocket of his tweed jacket for his cigar carrying case. ''For putting up with smoking in your house when lighting anything with tobacco in it has risen nearly to the level of a felony, I salute you. You're the solace of an old flatfoot's golden years.''

''She has no choice,'' said Kevin, giving Noreen a hug as Nick handed him a cigar and clipper. ''I told her before we got married that you'd thrown down a gauntlet. If she wanted our kids to get to know their grandfather, she'd have to get used to the smell of tobacco smoke when you came to the house.''

Nick stabbed the air with his cigar. ''That's a lie!''

''Actually I like cigars and pipes,'' Noreen replied as two Upmanns were lighted. ''My father smoked them all his life.''

''On every day of which, I'll bet,'' Nick said, assaying the status of a glowing end, ''your mother warned him, as Kevin's mother chided me, not to drop ashes on the rug.''

''Pop told her ashes were good for carpeting. He claimed they killed dirt mites.''

"Say, that's pretty good. I wish I'd thought of that. When I dropped ashes I made a beeline for the closet to get a broom and dustpan to get rid of the evidence."

Kevin tilted his head back and blew a column of smoke toward the ceiling. "I heard from a usually reliable source close to the Cambridge PD homicide squad that the only evidence found at the scene of the Rupert murder was ashes from two cigars."

Nick smiled. "Is that so?"

"It's what I was told. I haven't been able to confirm it. I also heard, but haven't been able to confirm, that on the basis of the ashes the investigation is proceeding on the theory that whoever did the killing must have been someone the antiques dealer knew and trusted. And that robbery wasn't the motive."

"The police deduce all that from cigar ashes? Impressive!"

Kevin's head came down. "I suspect they didn't deduce a damn thing on their own. I think they had the benefit of observations by an expert on both tobacco and homicide investigations."

"Maybe they called in the author of a famous monograph on the topic. He titled it "Upon the Distinction between the Ashes of the Various Tobaccos." He also pointed out to his associate that to the trained eye there is as much difference between the black ash of the Trichinopoly and the white fluff of bird's-eye as there is between a cabbage and a potato. I'll remember the name of the fellow in a minute."

Noreen asked, "Do you mean Sherlock Holmes?"

"Of course he does, honey," blurted Kevin. "He's being coy. It's an old cop's trick when dealing with a nosy reporter. The ducking, dodging, dissembling, diverting, and denying routine is so ingrained in him that he automatically goes into that mode even when the reporter happens to be his own son."

"Certainly there is no detective, real or fictional," Nick said, looking past Kevin to Noreen, "who is more associated with smoking than Sherlock Holmes. Take tobacco ashes. His observation of them proved decisive in the solution of several cases. Did you know that pipes appear in all but four of the sixty stories penned by Sir Arthur Conan Doyle?''

Kevin looked at his wife and rolled his eyes. ''See what I mean? Ducking and dodging.''

''Although Holmes smoked cigarettes and cigars,'' Nick went on determinedly, ''and kept a supply of cheap cigars at hand in a coal scuttle, the pipe was unquestionably his preference in pondering the intricacies of whatever problem presented itself. He is so associated with pipes that the Peterson Company of Dublin put out an entire series of them a few years ago, each one named after a character or object mentioned in Sherlock's cases.''

''Very amusing, Dad,'' said Kevin, ''but it was not Sherlock Holmes who pointed out to Jack Lerch that the cigars smoked in that antiques store Monday evening were Montecristo Churchills.''

Nick studied the lengthening ash of his Upmann. ''The Montecristo is an excellent cigar. Did your source indicate whether the ones smoked in Rupert's store were Dominican or Cuban?''

''My source did not,'' Kevin answered, ''but the source did say there was only one cigar butt in the ashtray.''

''Did your source provide an explanation of the significance of that fact? If it is a fact.''

Kevin sat up. ''Its meaning is clear. The killer took away the second cigar because it might have provided evidence.''

Nick resumed smoking. ''I doubt that even your sister could raise fingerprints from a cigar wrapper.''

''Not from the wrapper, Dad. Off the band.''

''That's very good. I hadn't thought of that.''

Kevin sank back on the couch and snorted a laugh. ''The hell you hadn't!''

Nick's eyes shifted again to Noreen. ''You said that you like the smell of cigars and pipes. I doubt you would have cared for Sherlock's tobacco. He smoked a very nasty shag.''

Enjoying Nick's toying with her husband, Noreen asked, ''What about Dr. Watson? What did he smoke?''

''He spoke of smoking a type known as ship's, which

was a cheap but powerful kind of twisted plug. Later Holmes observed Watson smoking the Arcadia mixture of Watson's bachelor days. One may deduce from that reference that the good doctor had married a very remarkable woman.''

Amusement sparkled in Noreen's eyes. ''Remarkable? Why?''

''It is historical fact that, by and large, women have not been big fans of tobacco. That Watson continued to smoke after he married proves that Mrs. Watson did not object. It's also logical to assume that she let him smoke in their house.''

Kevin groaned. ''Ducking, dodging, and diversion!''

Tired of the game, Nick said, ''I appreciate the position you find yourself in, Kev. You're a reporter whose old man stumbled into a murder scene. That's a pretty good angle for your stories. But there is nothing more I can tell you that your source inside the police hasn't.''

''You could tell me why you were there.''

''As I told you on the phone, I'd gone there to see Rupert on a matter of business.''

''But you didn't tell me the nature of the business.''

''He wanted to sell me something.''

''When did you become interested in antiques?''

Nick chuckled. ''Since the morning I looked into my bathroom mirror and realized I'd become one.''

## Thirteen

ON WEDNESDAY MORNING Sergeant Evert placed the three-page, single-spaced report on top of a stack of papers in the center of Lerch's desk. "Findings of the crime scene team."

Lerch fingered the papers and grimaced. "Summarize it for me, please, Sergeant."

"They found hundreds of fingerprints all over the place."

"All belonging to Rupert's well-heeled customers, no doubt. This is not a fingerprint case. A guy who takes his cigar with him is not a guy to leave his fingerprints behind. What about the weapon that was used?"

"There were plenty of knives, swords, letter openers, and other assorted things with blades. None had bloodstains."

"The murder weapon also went out the door."

Evert laid a single sheet of paper atop the others. "We also have the medical examiner's preliminary report."

"Let me guess. Cause of death was the big gash in the neck."

"There was also a deep stab to the right side of the back of the neck just above the shoulder."

Lerch made a fist of his right hand and raised it. "So what we have is a right-handed killer standing in back of the antiques dealer and beginning his attack by stabbing, probably aiming for the back. But he missed."

"There is hope for us in that," said Evert excitedly. "A stab wound spurts blood. The clothing around the hand holding the knife would be spattered with it."

"Clothing that the killer got rid of as soon as he finished washing his hands," Lerch said, still looking at his upraised fist. "Rupert jumps up. The killer grabs him under the chin with his left hand and slashes the throat left to right. What's the ME say about the slash wound?"

"He figures it was made with a tip that was double-edged. It was a long blade." He picked up the autopsy report and scanned it quickly. "Seven or eight inches. The dimension and shape of the stabbing wound in the back of the neck suggests a lengthy blade that would have a shaft no wider than an inch. Possibly triangular in shape, ending in a hilt and with a heavy handle."

Lerch lowered his fist. "We are sure as hell not talking about a switchblade or pocket knife. This was not your average multipurpose knife. It was intended for cutting through flesh."

"Like a hunting knife?"

"The average hunter's knife is shorter with a broader blade. I doubt it was Rupert's friends who killed the animals whose stuffed heads were staring at me from the wall in Rupert's store. I can't see a bunch of college profs tramping around in the woods in the Berkshires. Time of death?"

"Between six and eight o'clock," Evert said, returning the autopsy report to the desk.

Lerch asked, "What about the search of Rupert's house?"

"The crime scene team gave it a good going over all day yesterday and came up with nothing."

Lerch bolted to his feet. "You head over to Cowperthwaite Street and do some poking around yourself. Look for anything with names. An address book. Christmas card list!"

"I believe Rupert was Jewish."

"Some of my best friends are Jewish. That doesn't keep them from sending cards, although the ones they mail out usually say 'Season's Greetings,' 'Happy Holidays.' While you're doing that I'm going to have a talk with another geezer to see what I can pick up that might provide a lead on a motive.''

While appreciating that writing reports and piling up paper for the file constituted for the detective the gravel and cement that formed the foundation of a successful case, especially in a homicide with even a hint of mystery to it, Jack Lerch had never relished doing so. Since day one as the head of his own squad he had demonstrated a need to get out of the office and into motion. Solving a homicide within forty-eight hours was not simply a rule of thumb. It was the first commandment.

To keep it you had to be like a hound in a fox chase. It meant getting off your rump, out of the kennel, and on the trail of your quarry as quickly as Jack jumped over the candlestick.

Unfortunately, he had mentioned the nursery rhyme to explain his homicide-solving philosophy to a newspaper reporter, who had pinned to him in print the nickname that had stuck to his back for nearly two decades: ''Nimble Jack.''

But through the years it had been demonstrated ability and not good fortune that resulted in what might have been a humiliating sobriquet becoming an accolade. His first solo case, the murder of Paulie Russo, was closed in a day and a half.

The next year, the killing of a Brink's armored truck guard in a shootout in front of a bank in Inman Square was resolved in a mere thirty hours. Numerous drug-related homicides were cleared up almost instantly.

His biggest coup of all, the kidnapping and murder of six-year-old Bobby Vane, was wrapped up in three days, which was soon enough in anybody's judgment to more than satisfy the first commandment of police work. But even more importantly, it validated that in the city of Cambridge, Massachusetts, there could be no getting away with murder.

This did not by any stretch of a newspaperman's imagination mean that in his zeal to live up to his image as Jack the Nimble and Jack the Quick, he was prepared to rely only on instinct and go crashing around a homicide case like the proverbial bull in the china shop.

Certainly there was in most investigations the need to proceed slowly. To collect the evidence ploddingly. To quell gut feelings and sift the clues. To go painstakingly. To interview witnesses. And interview them again. To give the forensic experts plenty of elbow room and enough time. To prepare and comb through written reports and files.

He was not, after all, the Sherlock Holmes of Cambridge. Nimble Jack was good. Very good, in fact. But he had yet to rush into a complicated homicide expecting to solve it with the same alacrity he had shown in the Bobby Vane case.

Nor in any of his cases had he flung himself flat onto his belly with a magnifying glass in hand. Why, he didn't even own one. But there was something thrilling in the ringing of his home telephone, as had happened Monday night when he was about to sit down for dinner, that stirred in him an impulse to race out into the night.

Forced by dense and tedious Massachusetts Avenue traffic to drive slowly, he passed Rupert's antiques store and saw nothing to indicate to passersby that it had been the scene of what newspaper stories had termed a brutal murder, as though there could be any other kind.

# Fourteen

STEPPING FROM THE Happy Smoking Ground, Nick watched with amusement as Lerch claimed an advantage of his job by parking his plainclothes car without fear of being ticketed for taking space next to a fire hydrant. "Hello, Jack," he called as Lerch exited the car. "If you're dropping in on Woolley, he's waiting for you in the store. He's been here since I opened at eight o'clock."

"That's terribly considerate of him," Lerch said, barging around Nick. "Dare I ask who tipped him off that I'd be wanting to talk with him?"

"The gentleman was not only a friend of the victim in your case, Jack," Nick said, following Lerch to the door, "he is a professional mystery writer. He's been expecting you to grill him since yesterday morning. He's looking forward to it. You could say it's a case of life imitating art!"

Entering the store, Lerch found Woolley standing next to the cash register. "Good morning, Professor. How are you today?"

Woolley straightened to his imposing full height. "For a man of my age, I'm thrilled to be alive."

"I'm sure you've got lots of years yet before God calls."

"How long I live has nothing to do with a deity. Life span is entirely a matter of genetics, luck, and the good sense to be careful crossing streets. A glass or two of amiable spirits each day has also proved beneficial." With a mischievous wink in Nick's direction, he added, "Nor must one overlook the salutory effects of fine tobacco."

"Be that as it may," said Lerch, "can I have a few minutes of your time?"

"As much as you need."

Lerch shot a glance at Nick. "Privately?"

"If I've learned anything in the course of my years," said Woolley, fishing in the pocket of his tweed jacket for his new pipe, "it's that the definition of a fool is the individual who talks to a detective investigating a homicide without a witness to the conversation. I am willing to answer whatever questions you have as long as Nick is present. Or am I under arrest?"

"Of course not."

"Am I a suspect?"

"No."

"I'm surprised and extremely disappointed. May I ask why I have been eliminated?"

"All the evidence points to the perpetrator being a younger man. He exhibited a great deal of strength in committing the act and a lot of speed in leaving the scene. He also smoked cigars. You obviously prefer a pipe."

"I can point out flaws in your thinking, Detective. But you are correct in reaching the conclusion that I'm not a murderer."

"Being a mystery writer, you'll appreciate that the way to begin investigating a murder in which there appears to be no obvious suspect is by getting to know the victim. And people who knew him. I understand you knew Stanley Rupert a very long time."

"When I was a youth the phrase was 'Since Hector was a pup.' I don't know what people say today when they mean a very lengthy period."

Nick puffed smoke. "My son measures time from the date of the Nixon Watergate scandal. Everything is dated before Woodward and Bernstein or after."

Lerch asked Woolley, "Did Stanley Rupert have a large circle of friends?"

"It was a rapidly shrinking one. It seems that not a year goes by in which I'm not called upon to attend a funeral, or to make arrangements for one. But it's not Stan's friends you wish to know about, is it? You're interested in his enemies. Did you note my use of the plural, Detective?''

"I hear very well. Did he have a lot of enemies?''

"It's been my experience that anyone who reaches seventy can not have done so without offending several individuals somewhere along the way.''

"I need specifics.''

"On that score I'm afraid I can't help you. The only person I knew who was at all antagonistic to Stanley Rupert died several years ago while vacationing at Barnstable. He tumbled out of a boat and was lost in the bay. If Stanley had other enemies, he never made them known to me. He was always secretive.''

"When did you first get to know him?''

"I met Stanley during the war. That's the Second World War. We renewed our friendship when I came to study medieval history at Harvard in 1947. I'd discovered a fascination for the subject while liberating Europe. All those Gothic cathedrals. All those illuminated manuscripts. Museums filled with suits of armor and coats of arms. When I arrived at Harvard, Stanley was already enrolled in the history department. Our meeting was a chance one, on a rainy day in the stacks of the Widener. That's when I found out Jerome Lazarus was also here. By the way, he's gone missing.''

Lerch's bushy eyebrows arched. "Excuse me?''

Nick interjected, "Jerome Lazarus. He's left town.''

Woolley poked Nick's shoulder rebukingly with the bit of the pipe. "The man has gone *missing*.''

Nick shook his head. "There is no evidence to support that he's done anything except go away for a couple of days.''

Woolley huffed and jammed the pipe into his breast pocket. "Pardon me, Nick,'' he said angrily, "but Detective Lerch is here to question *me*.''

"Okay, Professor,'' Nick replied. "Tell the story your way.''

Eyes alight, the old man spun a tale as enthralling as any

of his Inspector Jake Elwell novels. The mysterious encounter between Rupert and Lazarus at the Widener. The meeting that was to have unfolded that afternoon at four in Rupert's store. Rupert being murdered the very next night. On Tuesday Lazarus's cancellation of seminars. The janitor's report of two packed bags. Lazarus's early departure. The limousine.

Having listened impassively to this remarkably spellbinding narrative without a last chapter, Lerch said, "Well, Professor, as Nick said, there's really no evidence that Jerome Lazarus has gone, as you say, *missing*. It seems to me that he's simply gone away on a trip."

"Can't you see, Detective," Woolley exclaimed, "that Rupert's death and Lazarus's disappearance are related events?"

"Are you proposing that Lazarus murdered Rupert?"

"Ridiculous! Lazarus did not have the requisite strength to cut a man's throat. Even a seventy-four-year-old's."

"Then what are you saying?"

"That Lazarus knows who did it and is terrified he's next."

"Leaving this total speculation aside for the moment," said Lerch, "what can you tell me about Rupert's other acquaintances?"

"I can give you a list of persons I'm planning to notify about the memorial service."

"When will it be held?"

"The date has not been determined. I am in the process of completing the list. I can bring you a copy this afternoon."

"No need for you to go to all that trouble," Lerch said as he left the store. "I'll have it picked up."

Chewing his pipe and looking through the bay window as Lerch drove away, Woolley said to Nick, "I'm deeply worried about that man's ability to solve this case. He lacks the singular quality that separates a policeman from a great detective. Imagination."

As he spoke, two young men entered the store.

"What a pity it is," Woolley continued, "that Nick Chase is not investigating this affair."

With eyes on the men studying cigars in the showcase near the door, Nick stepped out from behind the register. "I deal in smoke. And I have customers."

# Fifteen

The next morning Peg Baron phoned as Nick was shaving. In keeping with her custom of dispensing with the amenities of beginning a phone conversation with small talk, she got right to the point. "You are joining me for dinner, Nick. Tonight! I will accept no excuses! You can get Sam Gargan or Professor Woolley to mind the damn store."

"What's so special about tonight?"

"Wilhelm Wieder wants to meet you."

"What the hell for?"

"He wants to thank you for the gift of the cigars."

"Gift? Where'd he get that idea?"

"From me."

"Why am I not surprised?"

"I just could not bring myself to ask him for the money, so I told him they were from an admirer, namely you."

"You know what you are, babe? You're a nut case. First you give two boxes of my Montecristos to some kid piano player, and now you expect me to have dinner with him. Next you'll want me to pick up the check."

"No, no, no. He's paying."

"Where's this dinner party to be? At one of those highbrow joints on Beacon Hill?"

"It's definitely your kind of place, Nick. We've got a

reservation for three at eight o'clock at the Union Oyster House.''

About halfway between the new federal government building and the old elevated expressway that had been renamed for John Fitzgerald Kennedy, the three-story brick building at 41 Union Square had witnessed much of the history of Boston and the United States while hosting at its bar and dining tables many of the people who had shaped it. Yet the Union Oyster House had stood steadfast and unfazed as the surrounding city transformed its low profile of flat rooftops to one of soaring skyscrapers, so that Nick had no difficulty imagining that through the door at any moment Daniel Webster would appear in search of a hot toddy, his face still flushed from debating the ownership of a foolish man's very soul with the Devil himself. Or James Michael Curley, the Boston mayor who was elected governor of the Commonwealth of Massachusetts and mayor again before he was convicted of mail fraud. Or a skinny ex-skipper of a sunken PT boat, fresh from becoming a hero in the Pacific, campaigning in 1946 for Congress from the Eleventh District, as safe a place for a Democrat as any in Boston, even without being bankrolled by his father Joseph P. Kennedy's seemingly bottomless pocketbook.

Contradicting all Nick's expectations that the pianist would be short, pudgy, and soft, Wilhelm Wieder was tall, slender, and athletic-looking. Fingers of the hand he offered in greeting fit the stereotype of the pianist, but while they were long and supple their grip was tight and strong. A vision of every note of Tchaikovsky's first piano concerto accompanied by the proud, wild shaking of a lion's mane was shattered by black hair as short as Sam Gargan's.

Anticipating the accents of a European, Nick heard precise English. ''Good evening, Mr. Chase. I feel I already know you.''

''People who do call me Nick.''

With a slight bow Wieder said, ''My friends call me Will.''

As they waited for dinner to be served, a waiter set

glasses of white wine before Peg and Wieder and a Dalwhinny single-malt scotch in front of Nick.

Raising his glass, Nick glanced at Peg's worried face and said, "Here's to music."

After a sip of wine, Wieder said, "A man who offers such a toast either appreciates music or is being extremely courteous."

"I make courtesy a general practice," said Nick with a smile. "But I also appreciate good music."

"Ah, *good* music! There's a subject we could spend all night debating beside a roaring fire as we drink superb cognac and smoke good cigars, no?"

"I'm afraid a debate with me on the subject of good music would be one-sided in your favor."

Wieder leaned forward excitedly. "But not if the subject for debate were cigars!"

"A man who wants Montecristos two boxes at a time," Nick retorted, "also knows a thing or two about cigars."

Wieder sat back. "You were overly generous in considering them a gift. But I must insist on paying."

Glancing at Peg, Nick picked up his drink. "Nonsense. A gift is a gift is a gift."

With a shrug of broad shoudlers, Wieder said, "Perhaps we could limit a debate about what you consider good music if you told me what you don't like."

After a sip of scotch, Nick declared, "I definitely do not like harpsichords."

Wieder laughed. "That's a start. What bothers you about the harpsichord?"

"The damn things sound like a load of tin tumbling down a flight of steps."

"I hope you think better of the piano."

"It depends who's got his hands on the keyboard."

"Who are your favorite pianists?"

"I'm very fond of Duke Ellington. And Art Tatum, of course."

"Ah! You are an enthusiast of jazz of an earlier era."

Nick toyed with his scotch. "That earlier era is the one in which I spent my youth. Or perhaps misspent it by sneaking into jazz clubs such as the Three Deuces, Famous

Door, and the Onyx on a block of West Fifty-second Street.''

''Swing Street!''

''That's what they called it. You do know your jazz.''

''I envy you your youth, Nick. Alas, my exposure to the jazz greats of that period is limited to recordings. Fortunately for me, jazz has always been popular in Paris, where I was raised.''

''I assumed from your name that you were born in Germany or perhaps Austria.''

''My grandfather was German. He was killed in the war. To get away from the Russians my grandmother emigrated to France with a son who would become my father. Thank God she did!''

''So your passport is French.''

''British, actually. My father married an English woman he met in Paris. They were both working for an international agency concerned with lingering issues of persons displaced during the war. Tracing and reuniting families, restitution of property, and so forth. My parents settled in London when I was twelve. So that explains why I and my younger brother Friedrich are now subjects of the British crown. Getting back to jazz. For a brief time I considered taking it up as a career.''

''What prevented you?''

''My father. Because he was financing my musical education, at considerable sacrifice on his part, I followed the classical route. It was he who changed the family name so mine would fit on concert hall billboards.''

Peg interjected excitedly, ''I'm hoping that I can get Nick to attend one of your recitals. I invited him to the performance of the Tchaikovsky, but he had another engagement Monday night. He wound up finding a man who'd been murdered.''

''Peg told me you found the body of that man who was killed in that store across the street from Harvard! When I read of it in the newspapers I was very upset. My brother is a student at Harvard. The idea there was a crazed killer in the neighborhood was a terrible shock. But what a horrendous experience it must have been for you, Nick, finding that fellow's body.''

Before Nick could answer Peg exclaimed, ''Nick will never admit this to anyone, but I'm sure his discovery was like being on a busman's holiday.''

Wieder frowned. ''I'm sorry. I don't understand.''

Peg's voice lowered to the whisper of a gossipy school-girl. ''Nick used to be the best homicide detective in New York City.''

''Is that so, Nick? You don't look a bit like my picture of a policeman.''

Nick took a sip of scotch. ''What's a policeman look like?''

''I take your point. One should not stereotype people.''

Peg said, ''If Nick were in charge of investigating the murder of Stanley Rupert, we'd all know very quickly who did it. And why.''

''But I thought that was known,'' said Wieder. ''The newspapers said it was robbery.''

''That's the official police version,'' Peg said. ''But Nick recognized immediately that it wasn't.''

''That's amazing,'' said Wieder. ''Are you allowed to tell me how you knew? Or must that remain a police secret?''

Nick smiled tightly. ''I'm not with the police.''

Peg sighed. ''More's the pity.''

As a waiter delivered three plates of oysters on the half shell, Nick gave her a rebuking look. ''Can we leave the subject of murder for another time and take advantage of the R in the month by devouring these scrumptious-looking bivalves?''

After two hours of table talk on every subject but murder, Nick offered a parting wave at Wieder as the pianist's cab drove away from the restaurant. Turning to Peg, he glowered. ''You were out of line in telling him robbery was not the motive. That fact is not for public consumption.''

A flicker of anger crossed her face. ''Then you shouldn't have said anything to me about it.''

Nick drew a cigar from a pocket case. ''And that crack

about a busman's holiday was embarrassing.''

Curling an arm around his waist as he held a match to his cigar, she said, "What's so embarrassing about it? It's true. And don't for one second try to convince me you didn't wish it were your case to handle."

"That's baloney, Peg," he said as they walked toward the lot where he had parked his car. "I left policing behind fifteen years ago with no regrets."

"Now who's slicing baloney? You did not give it up because you wanted to. You quit because you couldn't stand being parked behind a desk. Face it, Nick. You're still a bloodhound. Everyone who knows you sees right through your pretense that you've lost the yen to sniff around for clues."

"Complete balderdash!"

"Then why do you keep your old badge framed on the wall in back of the cash register?"

"Firemen, private security guys, and school crossing guards wear badges. Cops carry *shields*."

"And why is your police revolver kept under the counter?"

"Strictly in case of a stickup."

"The man who never once fired his pistol when he was on the police force is prepared to blast away with it to keep somebody from heisting the day's proceeds of a tobacco store, and perhaps all the boxes of Havana cigars he can scoop up?"

Reaching the car, Nick dug in his coat pocket for keys. "The sale of Havanas has been illegal in this country since Kennedy slapped a trade embargo on Cuba in 1962. Although not, I hasten to add, until after he'd sent Pierre Salinger out to stock the Oval Office humidor with a thousand H. Upmanns."

"There you go, resorting to your trick of changing the subject from something you don't care to discuss. I started out talking about you and all of sudden I'm being lectured on a ban on Cuban cigars."

"You're the one who mentioned them."

"When you thought Wieder was about to press you for

details of the murder, you quickly switched the subject to oysters.''

Unlocking the passenger door, Nick scowled. ''I thought our purpose in going to the Union Oyster House, aside from Wieder thanking me for cigars he thinks were a gift, *was* oysters.''

''It was obvious through the entire meal that our young host wanted to know more of your thoughts about the murder, but you had him so intimidated he was terrified that if he brought the subject up you'd snap his head off.''

''Murder should not be served as an oyster side dish.''

''You know why you're so testy tonight as well as I do,'' she said as she settled into the car and fastened the seatbelt. ''It's because you really *are* frustrated that it's not you investigating a murder in which the victim was a friend and customer.''

Nick snorted a laugh. ''It's you who should be grinding out paperback mysteries, not Roger Woolley.''

''Since you found Rupert's body you've been just like an old police dog straining at the leash. But all you can do is let out your frustration by barking at me.''

After a long weighty silence, Nick looked at her with pleading eyes. ''Care to stop in at my place for a nightcap?''

Studying her watch, she answered icily. ''It's late.''

Nick squeezed the steering wheel.''Ah! I'm being punished.''

''Not at all. I'm used to your baying. I've got to study the score of the Vivaldi Concerto in C Major for Diverse Instruments. The BSO is performing it Saturday night. I've got a solo.''

Nick barked, ''Well hooray for you.''

''But don't worry about being invited,'' she said sharply. ''It has a whole lot of harpsichord.''

Fifteen minutes later, lights in Woolley's apartment windows suggested Jake Elwell was at work on a case. Muffled chattering of a typewriter seemed to confirm it as Nick opened the door to his own apartment. Entering it and throwing a switch that turned on a lamp next to the couch, he looked poutingly across the room.

The result of a pointless spat over a piano player was having a nightcap by himself.

Because he had had scotch at dinner and followed a policy of not switching from one kind of alcohol to another the same evening, he poured Johnnie Walker Red halfway up an old-fashioned glass and carried it to the chair in which he customarily did his reading.

Next to a small humidor, the choices awaiting him atop an end table as he sank into the chair's softness with his legs stretched out included the latest edition of *Cigar Smoker*. The cover showed the grinning face of a handsome movie actor he had never heard of, who looked much too young to be allowed to put a lighted cigar into his dazzlingly toothy mouth. Beside the magazine lay a thick biography of Theodore Roosevelt that Jean had recommended and a history of the climactic Battle of the Bulge in which his Uncle Bob had been a participant. And there was *Game, Set, Match, Murder*. Jake Elwell's new mystery, it began with the discovery of the bludgeoned corpse of a Harvard professor on a public tennis court. That the man banging the typewriter upstairs had started writing it after a Sunday dinner at the home of Kevin and Noreen Chase accounted for the scene of the crime resembling the courts opposite their house. Setting aside the scotch, Nick lifted from the humidor an Arturo Fuente Brevas Royal. Short and mild, it was the ideal late-night accompaniment to fine liquor and a good book, especially for a man left alone.

Alternately sipping and puffing, he reached chapter eight with an inkling as to who had bashed Randolph Roberts over the head with a tennis racquet. Then he became aware that the muted sounds of typing heard through the ceiling had been replaced by rapping on the apartment door.

As he opened it, Woolley barged in. "I knocked earlier but you weren't home. I've been waiting for you for hours."

Nick spoke through a puff of smoke. "I was out with Peg."

"I know. That's why I was afraid you'd stay out all

night. Or that Peg would come back here. But when I smelled your cigar I knew you were home at last. And alone.''

''Would you care to explain?''

''You refrain from smoking as much when she is here.''

''That's not what I meant. Why were you waiting for me?''

''It concerns Jerome Lazarus. But you must see for yourself.'' Nick puffed again and shut the door. ''Suppose you tell me.''

''Very well,'' said Woolley from the center of the room. ''He did not, as you would have me believe, simply *go away*.''

Returning to his chair, Nick put the cigar in an astray. ''So we're back to that again.''

''It's as I surmised,'' Woolley said, urgently grasping Nick's arms. ''He's fled in terror. I have the proof.''

''What proof? Show me. I don't want theories. I'm not a bit interested in interpretations, Professor. It's late, I've had a row with Peg, I'm tired, and I have to be up early.''

''To see the proof,'' said Woolley, releasing his strong grip on Nick's arms, ''you must accompany me to his apartment.''

Nick looked down at the unfinished cigar, drink, and book. ''You mean *now*?''

''Certainly now. A life is at stake.''

Nick retrieved the cigar. ''Go to the police. Call Lerch. I'm going to bed.''

Woolley threw up his arms. ''That man is pathetic. He's too closeminded to understand anything.''

''That's nonsense.''

''Nonsense, is it? May I remind you that if it weren't for your observations Monday night Lerch and his minions would be looking for a nonexistent robber, and despite all your brilliant deductions probably is? It is now up to you to show Lerch that he should be searching for someone who murdered once and is likely to kill again. How can you even think of going to bed?''

''How do you propose we get into Lazarus's place? In

addition to being an expert on how to murder people are you also a second-story man?''

''I certainly know how to pick a lock,'' Woolley boasted.

''Breaking and entering,'' said Nick, ''is a felony.''

''Resorting to criminality won't be required,'' Woolley said as he patted a pocket. ''I have a key.''

''How convenient!''

''People of a certain age, living alone and without a family, take precautions,'' Woolley said while Nick put on a light jacket. ''One of them is to arrange for a trusted friend to check on you from time to time to make sure you're all right. And if you have not been seen around lately to find out if you are ill, and to see if you are still alive. You're lucky on that score. You've got your children. Your employees, Sam Gargan and Craig Spencer. Myself. Plus Peg Baron, of course. In my case it is you. But before you moved in downstairs it was Lazarus and Rupert.''

''Having a key to Lazarus's apartment doesn't bestow on you the right to enter it when he's not there,'' Nick said as they descended the stairs, ''and you know why he isn't at home.''

''We've been over that, Nick. Lazarus has disappeared because he fears for his life.''

''That is the romantic imagination of a mystery writer.''

''It is a cruel fact which *you* will verify when you've been to his apartment,'' Woolley said as they left the building. ''No need to use your car. It's just a few blocks' walk.''

After a glance confirmed that the imperiled wooden Indian was still in place, Nick fell in step with Woolley's brisk pace. Retracing the route Woolley had taken on the day he learned from the janitor of Lazarus's abrupt departure in a limousine, they came to the Chapman Arms Apartments. Imagining its residents asleep behind the darkened windows of the gray block silhouetted against a black sky, Nick muttered, ''This is downright insanity!''

Woolley huffed. ''Nonsense. Come along.''

''We are going to get kicked out on our keisters.''

''The secret to not getting kicked out,'' Woolley replied

as he pushed open the lobby door, "is to look as if you belong."

Encountering no one to question their presence in the lobby or in an elevator, they arrived at Lazarus's floor.

Taking the key from his pocket, Woolley whispered, "Now you will see for yourself why I am convinced Lazarus did not simply go traipsing off on a whim and a lark."

As Woolley opened the door wide and a shaft of light spilled from the hall into a dark living room, Nick muttered, "Holy cow. It looks like a tornado ripped through here."

"It was a tornado all right," said Woolley with vindication in his voice. "A human one. If you didn't before, you now know the meaning of 'ransacked.' Everything is exactly the way I found it this afternoon."

"Professor, you should have called the police."

"I thought it important that you see all this first."

"Okay, I've seen it. *Now* call the police."

"You know as well as I do what will ensue. A couple of cops in uniform will arrive, look around, and conclude that somebody learned Lazarus left carrying suitcases and then took advantage of the opportunity to burglarize his apartment."

"It's a very logical deduction. Years ago I worked a case in which a crew of alert thieves watched a family leave for what was obviously going to be an extended vacation and pulled up the next day with a huge truck disguised as a moving van and carted off the entire contents of the house."

"Be that as it may, this mess was not the work of an alert burglar. What second-story men have you known who ransacked the premises? They open drawers and closets. They grab what they can in a hurry and run. They don't hang around to savage the place."

"This is evidently an exception to the rule. Shall you call the police, or must I?"

# Sixteen

THE NEXT MORNING Detective Jack Lerch propped big feet on top of his desk, folded pudgy hands on his plump belly, and smiled at Nick like the Cheshire Cat. "You know as well as I do that Lazarus messed up his apartment himself. I can't believe you went hook, line, and sinker for Woolley's theory that Lazarus took off because he was afraid whoever killed Stanley Rupert was out to get him, too."

Nick fished his cigar case from a pocket and an Upmann from the case. "Who says Lazarus didn't take off for that reason?"

"I had Evert check out the limousine services. The records of the one Lazarus hired show he booked a car the day *before* the murder. He also bought a one-way ticket from a commuter airline."

"Going where?"

"Provincetown."

"Did he actually use the ticket?"

"Yes. I've got police down there trying to locate him. And if he's there, they will find him, and then he'll asked to explain how a man who made plans on a Sunday to leave town on Tuesday could believe he was next in line for murder when Rupert was killed *Monday* night."

"He could have had an inkling Rupert was going to die."

Lerch laughed. "An *inkling*? From whence came this inkling?"

"Sacrcasm doesn't become you, Jack."

"If Lazarus had an inkling, why didn't he come to us, or at least warn Rupert?"

"Perhaps he did but Rupert didn't take him seriously."

Lerch removed his feet from the desk and sat up straight. "I think what happened was that Lazarus killed Rupert and hoped to point the finger at someone else by wrecking his apartment to make it look as if the person who killed Rupert had come looking for him. He knew Professor Woolley would get worried and sooner or later go to his apartment, find it in a wreck and jump to the conclusion Lazarus was hoping for. Lazarus's expectation was that if he made it look as though his apartment was ransacked we would be deflected into looking at him as a potential victim, rather than as a suspect. That gave him time to fly the coop."

"Which he seems to have done rather ineptly," Nick said as he took matches and a clipper from a pocket.

"Sorry, Nick," said Lerch with a worried look. "Smoking is not permitted on city property, even in private offices."

With a scowl, Nick returned cigar to case, and case, matches, and clipper to pockets. "If your theory of the case is Lazarus killing Rupert I'm afraid it doesn't wash."

"With respect, Nick, I believe it does."

"Do you agree that two cigars were smoked in Rupert's office immediately before he was killed?"

"As you pointed out Monday night, the killer smoked one with Rupert and then took it with him."

"Lazarus was not a smoker. His doctor made him give it up a couple of years ago."

Lerch waved a dismissing hand. "Another deflection. Lazarus smoked a cigar to mislead our investigation."

"Impossible. The cigars that were smoked were Montecristos taken from the box in Rupert's office. Rupert would not give a cigar to a man he knew didn't smoke. Yet two of the Montecristos were taken from the box and smoked in that office."

"Rupert could have had one of them earlier in the day."

"Where were the remains of the earlier one?"

"He could have smoked it somewhere else. On the street!"

"Highly unlikely, Jack."

"I see guys on the streets smoking cigars all the time."

"I've sold Stanley Rupert cigars for fifteen years. He's a connoisseur. He would never open a box of Montecristos on the street. You do that with a pack of Phillies or White Owls. A Montecristo is smoked indoors and at leisure. And even if Rupert did smoke the second Montecristo elsewhere, you still have to explain ashes from two Montecristos in the tray in his office. You can't have it both ways. If he opened the box of Montecristos before he got back to his store and smoked one of them somewhere else, how did the second Montecristo ash get in the tray?"

"There's no way to prove that second ash came from a Montecristo, is there?"

"If two cigars were smoked in the office before the murder, but only one was a Montecristo, where'd the second come from?"

"Lazarus brought it."

"Why?"

"As I said, it was to be a diversion."

"No, Jack. The second ash in the tray came from the second Montecristo. Since it was smoked in the office, it couldn't have been Lazarus who smoked it. That eliminates him as a suspect."

Lerch's expression soured. "So you say."

"I do and I will, unless you have solid evidence to prove that I'm wrong. Do you?"

Lerch shifted uneasily in his chair. "Not yet. All we've got is a bunch of worthless fingerprints lifted in Rupert's store."

"As you'd expect in a place open to the public."

"And no weapon has turned up, probably because it's been swimming with the fishes in the Charles since Monday night."

"What did you find out about all that money you uncovered in Rupert's desk drawer?"

"He withdrew it from his bank Monday morning. On the

form he had to fill out he said it was to buy a manuscript from a private party who insisted on getting cash. No way to check that out. As far as we know he could have needed the cash because he was being blackmailed, or to pay off a bookie. I'd look around for a lady or even a boyfriend if Rupert wasn't in his seventies.''

''I see the behavior gestapo who banned smoking at police headquarters still has a good deal of educating to do with you in other areas. I believe the politically correct definition of the crime you have just committed is *ageism*. But don't worry, Jack, I won't turn you in. I am not nor have I ever been a quisling.''

Blushing, Lerch said, ''A what?''

''A quisling is a term from World War II. Well before your time, of course. The quislings were Nazi collaborators, what cops and the criminal class of today call informants.''

''I could sure use a snitch in this case. Even better, I'd like someone with a guilty conscience to come in and confess. I'm beginning to think that's what it's going to take if I'm going to close the book on this murder. Until you walked in I'd thought I was going to pin it on Lazarus.''

''I wouldn't stop looking for him. He may have taken off for the Cape because he does have an idea who killed Rupert. We still don't know why his apartment was turned upside down.''

''If Lazarus wasn't the killer—and I'm not conceding that point—maybe the killer was frustrated because Lazarus wasn't at home when he came calling.''

''He could have waited for Lazarus to come home. Instead he ripped the place apart and left. Why?''

Lerch joked, ''Maybe he lost something!''

Nick bolted forward in his chair. ''Jack, have your men checked Rupert's house to see if it was also searched?''

''I sent a crime scene team and Evert on that mission. They found the place locked up tight and neat as a pin.''

''That's strange,'' said Nick, sinking back. ''It seems to me it should have been as much a mess as Lazarus's apartment.''

''I'm listening.''

''Suppose this man did not go to see Rupert intending

to kill him, but to get Rupert to hand over whatever he was looking for. They talked. Smoked cigars. But Rupert couldn't be persuaded to give up whatever it was the man wanted. At that point, Rupert's visitor had enough of gentle persuasion and resorted to force. He grabbed a knife. There were plenty of them in that store. Then he held the knife to Rupert's throat until Rupert told him what he wanted to know. Rupert believed he could save himself by saying the object was in Lazarus's apartment. Instead he ended up with his throat slit.''

''But when the killer went to Lazarus's place and had a look around,'' Lerch said, ''he realized Rupert had lied to him.''

''This is all speculation, of course,'' Nick said as he got up to leave. ''Good luck getting to the bottom of this mess.''

Lerch demanded, ''Where are you going?''

''To a place where I'm allowed a cigar.''

Returning to The Happy Smoking Ground and finding Woolley smoking his pipe and engaged in conversation with Sam Gargan, Nick announced, ''Your friend Lazarus appears to have chosen to take his impromptu vacation on the Cape. Lerch's stalwart deputy, the intrepid Sergeant Gary Evert, has traced him to a commuter air service that took him to Provincetown.''

Woolley plucked the pipe from his mouth. ''Ha! Of course he did! I should have known Lazarus would pull a stunt like that.''

''Stunt?''

''Lazarus is *not* in Provincetown.''

Nick went behind the counter. ''That's what it said on the ticket he used Tuesday morning.''

''I have not said he did not *buy a ticket* to Provincetown. He did that to mislead anyone who might try tracing him. If he took such a flight at all he would have gotten off at Barnstable.''

Sam Gargan stepped forward. ''What's at Barnstable?''

''A summer cottage Lazarus has owned since he was mustered out of the army in 1946.''

"How could an ex-GI afford to buy a cottage in Barn-stable?"

"He didn't buy it, Sam. He had the foresight immediately after the war to purchase a small lot and build on it. If he is there now I hope he's taken his longjohns. The house has never had year-round heating. It may be spring, but the nights can still get very chilly down there. Of course, it's a very lovely spot in summertime. I vacationed there several times in the past fifty-odd years."

Nick looked sternly at Woolley. "Professor, you might have saved the police a good deal of trouble if you'd told Lerch about this cottage when Lerch questioned you."

"My dear Nick," said Woolley defensively, "it never occurred to me that Lazarus would go there. Yet now that it appears that he's done just that, it makes perfect sense."

Nick picked up the phone. "There's one way to find out."

With alarm Woolley demanded, "What are you doing?"

"I'm going to tell Lerch to contact the Barnstable police."

Wooley grasped Nick's hand. "Please don't. I've known this man for half a century. He did not go to the police after finding his apartment had been broken into and searched because he had a compelling reason not to."

Nick thought a moment, then cracked a slight smile. "Such as not having to tell the police what the intruder was looking for?"

Woolley lifted his hand off Nick's. "I believe if I were to talk with Lazarus he might not feel so reticent. At the moment he needs to confide in someone he can trust. Myself."

"If he's so trusting of you why didn't he come to you right away Tuesday morning?"

"I can only conjecture that he intended to contact me in due course. But only from a place of safety."

"I've known you for quite a while, Professor. I can almost see the plot wheels spinning in your brain. Out with it."

"This is a matter requiring the skills of an expert sleuth," Woolley said, jabbing the air with the bit of the pipe. "You must accompany me to Barnstable, Nick. There's not a moment to lose."

"I've got a store to run."

Woolley looped an arm around Sam Gargan's shoulders. "You have Sam for that," he said, giving the startled, slender youth a hug. "Having witnessed his deft handling of a recent customer, I can attest to his superb salesmanship. What is more, because you have been involved in this murder case from the very beginning, you have an obligation to see the investigation is not bungled."

"Lerch's investigation is coming along very well."

"I grant you the man is the best of the lot in the homicide squad. In run-of-the-mill murders he is commendably workmanlike. Unfortunately, in a case that is as complicated as this one he lacks the vision required. Would you entrust the delicate task of finding Lazarus to provincial police? I don't think so."

"If you're convinced Lazarus has holed up in Barnstable," Nick said, "there's an easy way to find out. Use my phone."

"If you believed you were being hunted, would you answer? The only way to know if Lazarus is in Barnstable is to go there. That leaves only one thing to be settled. Your car or mine?"

"Certainly not yours. I've seen how you drive."

# PART II

*Twilight of Idols*

# Seventeen

AFTER BRIDGING THE Cape Cod Canal, eastbound Route 6 coursed like an artery through the arm-shaped peninsula that bent its elbow at the town of Orleans and ended in a hand at Provincetown.

"I presume you've visited the Cape often," said Woolley.

"Kevin drags me to Yarmouth occasionally for fishing. And I went along once with him and Jean on a sightseeing outing to the Kennedy compound at Hyannisport. But I've never shared my kids' enthusiasm for sand dunes and salt air."

Woolley chuckled. "You can take the boy out of the city, but you can't take the city out of the boy, eh?"

"Something like that."

"I agree," Woolley said, looking through the windshield at glowering clouds that portended rain. "I am never comfortable removed from a decent library. That is not to say there are no good repositories of books in these parts. The Sturgis Library was established in 1644 in the town that is our destination. To get there we leave this highway at exit six."

"I know, Professor. I've looked at the map."

"As in most coastal settlements founded by religious-minded men in these parts," Woolley continued, "seafarers of Barnstable found no problem reconciling piety with profits from the evil of the trade triangle of molasses, rum, and slaves.''

"In other words, they were people of their times."

"My dear fellow, the pages of history are littered with examples of that dreary rationale for justifying winking at evil. It was the times. Everybody was doing it. I had my family to support. I was merely carrying out orders. We were *good Germans*. We didn't support the Nazis, but what could we do about them? Honest, Lieutenant, I had *no idea* Jews were being gassed.''

As huge raindrops splattered against the windshield, Nick asked, "Lieutenant who?"

"I beg your pardon?"

"You said, 'Honest, Lieutenant.' "

"You know that was my rank in the army during the war.''

"Yes, but I didn't know you were in the shooting war."

"Where did you think I was?"

"Behind the lines being brainy. A codebreaker!"

"I *was* in Army Intelligence, but as a debriefer. After a battle I interviewed captured troops. When we took a town I also questioned the residents. When we began liberating concentration camps it was survivors.'' His voice choked. "It was like talking with animated skeletons!"

Nick switched on windshield wipers. "I'm sorry for stirring bad memories.''

Woolley looked at him sidelong. "No apology needed. How could you know there were any memories to stir up?"

"My late brother-in-law was in the war. He drove a half-track in the Third Army.''

"One of Patton's boys? Old Blood and Glory, they called him. His glory, their blood.''

"What did you think of Eisenhower?"

"Ike as a general or Ike as President of the United States?''

"Both."

"I actually met General Ike once. He inspected one of the liberated concentration camps.''

"There I go again, stirring bad memories."

"It's all right. This is a better memory, actually. Ike did

what I'd been wishing I could have done. When he saw the horror of that particular camp, he ordered everyone in the closest town brought into the place to face what had been going on under their noses. That's when one of them told me he had no idea Jews were being gassed. The hell he didn't. As to Ike in the White House, the country could have done a whole lot worse. And probably no better. There's the sign for our turnoff.''

"From this point on," said Nick, "you're the navigator."

Following the curve of the old Route 6, now called 6A, they skirted marshland and dunes separating the road from the broad and broodingly dark surface of Cape Cod Bay, and passed through the quiet center of West Barnstable.

"In a couple of months," Woolley said, peering through the rain, "this scene will be alive with summer people in T-shirts, shorts, and sandals. Plus the antiques hunters. Rupert once played with the notion of opening a shop down here."

"Why didn't he?"

"One of the two partners he had in mind drowned in a boating mishap. After that tragedy the other one lost all interest. Not wanting to go it alone, Rupert gave up the idea. He was content to join the summer people by spending every August in Lazarus's hideaway cottage. The street sign to look for when we get into Barnstable itself is Mill Way. You hang a left."

Expecting a traditional Cape Cod–style house with gray or white clapboard sidings and a shingled roof pierced by a tall brick center chimney, Nick was surprised to find a steeply slanted roof jutting above a sandy ridge dotted with pines. Unpainted wooden walls of the A-frame house conveyed more of a mountain chalet than a house for seaside summering.

"It's a pity the weather has turned so beastly," Woolley said as Nick switched off the engine in front of the cottage. "The view of the harbor from Lazarus's rear deck on a sunny day is a spectacularly panoramic seascape."

Gazing at the house through a windshield rendered almost opaque by cascading rain, Nick said, "The place is dark. I have a feeling we've wasted the day on a wild goose chase.''

''If you believed a murderer was looking for you,'' Woolley said, stepping into the downpour, ''would you sit around waiting for him with the lamps on?''

Unmoving, Nick said, ''If he's in there, where's his car?''

''He doesn't drive,'' Woolley answered as he dashed toward the cottage. ''He would have hired a cab in Barnstable.''

Quickly getting soaked as he raced to join Woolley under the roof of a small, windowless porch, Nick grumbled, ''I really do not believe Lazarus is here.''

''He must be,'' Woolley replied, pounding on the solid door. ''Where else could he have gone?''

Wiping rain from his face, Nick retorted, ''The plane he got aboard on Tuesday was going to *Provincetown*.''

''The plane went there. Jerome Lazarus definitely did *not*. I am terribly concerned about this lack of response.''

''My friend, Lazarus is obviously not here,'' Nick said in exasperation, ''and you and I are very close to getting drowned.''

''I tell you there's no other place he would have gone.''

''It's a wide, wide world, my friend.''

''I have a very bad feeling about this, Nick. Someone was in Lazarus's apartment. That person may have known about this place. He could have followed Lazarus here. I'm afraid you are going to have to break in this door.''

With a sigh of frustration, Nick said, ''Why don't I go round to the side and find a window?''

''Capital idea! Perhaps one's been left unlocked.''

''I'm not going to break in. I'm going to *look* in. I haven't come down here to get arrested on a burglary charge.''

Finding a low window on the leeward side of the building, he peered past lace curtains, muttered ''Unholy hell,'' and broke the glass with an elbow. Reaching in, he released a lock and then opened the window. As he climbed through it, a gust of rainy wind caused the figure dangling from a rafter to sway slightly.

\*        \*        \*

On the dusty floor directly in front and slightly right of the body lay an overturned three-step, wooden library ladder.

Digging into the inside pocket of his jacket for his cell phone, Nick paused a moment to consider that for the second time in less than a week he was using it to report a dead man.

A moment later, Officer Mel Granick answered the call as if his name were Barnstable Police Granick.

Listening to Granick through the open door, Chief of Police Michael Ludlum heard: "What's that, sir? Someone's hanged himself? Where? The Lazarus cottage on Mill Way. Yes, I know the place. Tell me your name again? Okay. Remain there, Mr. Chase. Don't move the body. Don't touch a thing."

Seated beside Woolley on a pillowed settee as police took down the body, examined it, and removed it, Nick observed Ludlum survey the scene with impressive authority and professionalism.

When Ludlum disappeared into the kitchen, Woolley turned to Nick and whispered, "I knew Lazarus was desperate, but I never expected him to do this."

Emerging from the kitchen, Chief Michael Ludlum rubbed his jaw and looked at the men on the settee. "There is no doubting this was suicide."

Woolley shot to his feet. "Nonsense! Where is the note?"

Ludlum looked at the rafter where the rope had been looped. "Absence of a note is not unusual."

Woolley paced the room. "If he planned to kill himself, why did he go to the bother of packing a couple of suitcases and come all the way down here to do it?"

"We have no way of knowing that, Mr. Woolley. The suitcases only prove that he did not decide to take his life immediately. He thought about it for awhile. I've had a look around this cottage and I can confidently say that Mr. Lazarus didn't just walk in, throw a rope over a rafter, and hang himself. He'd been in this house for a couple of days.

He brought food. There are enough canned goods in the cabinet in the kitchen to last a week. He's slept in the bed. He took a shower today. A towel in the bathroom is still damp. All this shows he spent a lot of time here before he hanged himself. Do you concur, Mr. Chase?''

Nick shifted forward on the settee, clasped hands as if he were praying, and slowly nodded. "I do.''

"Is it not possible,'' Woolley said, looking between Nick and Ludlum angrily, "that someone else came into this house, *murdered* him, and arranged everything to look like a suicide?''

Ludlum scratched his chin. "I've found nothing to indicate that anything like that happened here.''

Woolley threw up his arms in disgust. "What would it take to overpower a man of Lazarus's age and physical condition? How much struggle would he be capable of?''

"Neither the body nor this room shows any signs of there being a struggle.''

"He could have been struck on the head.''

"I found no blood, no bruising.''

"He could have been strangled first and then hanged.''

"The only marks on the neck were made by the rope. There's also the matter of the placement of the ladder. You'll note that it's in a position suggesting he kicked it out from under him.''

"The ladder could have been easily arranged by the murderer to make it look as though Lazarus had kicked it away.''

Ludlum's face twisted almost as if he were in pain. "I don't believe that happened, Mr. Woolley.''

As Woolley turned pleadingly for a word of support, Nick left the settee to kneel and point to the floor beneath the spot where the body had hung. "To get Lazarus to this spot,'' he said, "the body would have to be dragged. There are no drag marks.''

"The body was carried!''

"As to the ladder,'' Nick continued, "examine the marks made in the dust by the tips of its legs. I would describe them as skid marks made when the ladder either slipped or was purposely kicked away. I am sorry, my friend, but this was a suicide.''

After a long silence, Woolley sighed and turned teary eyes up to the rafter. "I always knew Lazarus was a fool," he said as he returned to the settee, "but I never thought he was a man who would ultimately fall to pieces. Not after all this time.''

"I appreciate how upsetting this must be for you gentlemen," Ludlum said, "but there are a couple of questions I have to ask.''

"The first one being: Why are we here?" Nick said. "And the second: Do we have any idea why he would kill himself?''

"Those are good for starters," said Ludlum as he drew up a chair that looked old enough to have been brought from Rupert's stock of antiques. "If you lived here you wouldn't have had to enter this house by breaking a window. Nor does it appear, for the same reason, that your arrival was anticipated.''

Nick smiled appreciatively. "It's a long story.''

Ludlum reciprocated Nick's smile. "Stories that end with the police being called usually are. Take all the time you need.''

Telling him of the Rupert murder, the ransacked apartment, Lazarus's sudden departure on Tuesday, Woolley's deduction of his likely destination, and the various theories discussed with Lerch took ten minutes.

When he was sure Nick's narrative was finished, Ludlum said, "The murder of Rupert and the suicide of his closest friend seem to be more than a coincidence. What brings you to the conclusion Lazarus didn't kill Rupert and in a state of guilt and possibly fear of being caught, take the quick way out?''

"There are two reasons. One: Lazarus's physical condition. I can't see a man that frail cutting Rupert's throat. But he might have known, or suspected, who did. Second: Somebody searched his apartment. The two events sent Lazarus fleeing in fear.''

"It's a hell of an interesting case," Ludlum said. "But it's not mine. The time has come to advise my brother-in-crime Lerch what happened here. I wish him the best of luck in solving the case. And I wish the two of you a safe trip back to Cambridge, that is, after you've given one of my officers formal witness statements.''

# Eighteen

As Woolley settled morosely into the car, Nick said, "I'm sorry the day had to end this way, my friend."

"Now I've got two memorials to arrange. At this rate of demises there will be no one left of my generation to mark my own giant leap into oblivion."

"Assuming the Grim Reaper doesn't tap me on the shoulder first," Nick said, starting the car and thinking of the miles ahead to Cambridge and feeling relieved that the rain had dwindled to drizzle, "you can rely on me to bid you godspeed."

"You are hardly my generation. You're a veritable child."

"Baloney. You're only ten years older than me."

"Twelve."

Following Mill Way toward the center of Barnstable, Nick said, "It's not the years that matter, it's what you do with them. As the philosopher/comedian Fred Allen said, 'You only go around once in life, but if you do it right, once is enough.' "

Woolley stared straight ahead. "Years as they pass plunder us of one thing or another."

"Shakespeare?"

"Before the Bard of Avon's time there was Horace."

"Speaking of time," Nick said, executing a right turn from Mill Way onto 6A, "what did you mean when you said that you never thought Lazarus would ultimately fall to pieces, *not after all this time*?''

In a tone that seemed a little ruffled, Woolley blurted, ''I meant after so many days.''

''From Tuesday to Friday isn't all that many days.''

''I have no idea what you are getting at,'' Woolley snapped.

Startled, Nick asked, ''Why are you suddenly hot under the collar with me?''

''I do not appreciate my sentences composed in a moment of terrible shock and deep personal grief being parsed for possible significance in a presumed hidden subtext. And do not insult my intelligence by claiming it was not the intent of your question. You are on a fishing expedition. Very well, spit out whatever it is you have on your mind.''

''I was simply wondering if the hidden subtext, to use your phrase, was that you expected Lazarus to have been a candidate for suicide some time ago. And there was your other phrase, about Lazarus ultimately falling to pieces.''

''What about it?''

''You sounded to me as though you expected Lazarus to fall to pieces over something.''

''I was referring to his failing health.''

''Lazarus was ill?''

''Oh my yes. I feared he might try to end it all. Because he made no attempts, I was surprised that he would do so after all this time.''

''I'm sorry, perhaps I'm missing something. If you'd always feared his health might drive him to kill himself, why were you so adamant in insisting to Chief Ludlum that Lazarus had been murdered?''

''It's as you said. Rupert was murdered. Lazarus's apartment had been searched. He fled the city, obviously fearing he might be next. He was so frightened of being murdered—''

''That he went all the way to Barnstable to commit suicide? Come on, Professor, who's insulting whose intelligence now?''

''I find this conversation increasingly mystifying. If there is something troubling you, quit beating around the bush.''

''It's strictly conjecture, of course.''

"Out with it, man. Out with it!"

"Since the day after Rupert was murdered I've had a sinking feeling in my gut that you've not been straight with me."

"Not straight with you? About what?"

"About everything that's been going on, beginning the day after the Rupert murder when you went looking for Lazarus. Why did you feel you had to do that?"

"I was worried about him."

"Obviously. But why?"

"Rupert had been murdered."

"Why should that make you go looking for Lazarus?"

"He was Rupert's closest friend. He was also my dear friend. I thought I ought to be the person to tell him, and to be there for him. That's what friends do for one another."

"Yet you made no attempt to tell him of Rupert's death until a couple of hours after I'd told you about the murder."

"But I did. I phoned him immediately after you'd gone."

"There you go not being straight with me again. I informed you of the murder at six o'clock on Tuesday morning. If you had called him immediately, why would you go looking for him around eight? You waved at me through the window of my store as you were on your way to Harvard Yard."

"When Lazarus and I spoke on the phone we planned to meet later at his office."

"Impossible. Lazarus was not able to take your call at six o'clock. The janitor at his apartment told you Lazarus left in a limousine at five-thirty. What also puzzles me is why you insisted I be with you when you went to Lazarus's apartment, why I had to come with you today to Barnstable, and why you've been egging me on all along to get involved in the investigation of this case even more than I already was."

"I gather you've developed a theory."

"I wouldn't call it a theory."

"What would you call it?"

Nick thought a moment. "A concern. A concern that you know or suspect a good deal more about Rupert's murder and Lazarus's suicide than you hope I, and more importantly Jack Lerch, might find out. If that is true the time has arrived for you to quit stringing me along. If I am to be of any help, you have to confide in me.''

''That will require my summarizing another long story.''

''It's a long drive back to Cambridge.''

''It was April of 1945. The closing weeks of war in Europe. I was officer in charge of a group of four interrogators.''

''Let me guess. Two were Rupert and Lazarus.''

''Rupert was a sergeant, Lazarus a corporal, and Jonathan Little and Sid Gold privates. I was their lieutenant. We were with First Army, which, along with Patton's Third, was barrelling eastward into a zone of Germany the politicians had assigned to the Russians to capture and occupy. But our intelligence services tipped Eisenhower's staff that in the area around Gotha there was a salt mine, two thousand feet deep, full of gold bullion and art and other treasures looted by the Nazis. The estimated value was a quarter of a billion dollars.''

Nick let out a whistle.

''It turned out to be a great deal less than that, but it was an incredible trove. After Eisenhower, Patton and my own First Army's General Omar Bradley inspected the mine, they went to inspect a nearby liberated concentration camp by the name of Ohrdruf Nord.''

''This is the camp that so revolted Ike he forced Germans in the town to see what had happened there?''

''Correct. It was so bad that even Georgie Patton threw up. But the day before the generals' inspection I was ordered to take my group and get to the camp ahead of the brass in case one of the generals wanted to talk to victims. Just as today when we smelled the sea before we saw the bay, we could smell death in the air long before we reached the camp. But about a mile or two before we got there, we were surprised as hell to see a Nazi officer rushing out of a barn and headed in our direction, his arms upraised and waving a white handkerchief. When Rupert took away his Luger you never saw so happy a Nazi in your life. He had been terrified we were Russians. He was a captain in the SS with one of those long, funny-sounding German last names. I got a kick calling him the name of one of Red Skelton's radio characters, Clem Kadiddlehopper. Little got a boot out of that, too. But not Rupert and Gold. Being Jewish, they were not amused. They wanted to ignore the regulations that said officers of his rank and over were to be interrogated. They wanted to shoot him. And they might have if Kadiddlehopper hadn't started ranting on about a treasure he had. He said if we freed him we'd divide it six ways.''

''You believed him?''

''Of course not. But then he told me to search his pockets. He said I'd find a map. Sure enough, there it was.''

Nick barked a laugh. ''He actually had a *treasure* map?''

''I know this sounds ludicrous, Nick, but the map even had the location marked with an X. While I was studying it, Kadiddlehopper threw up his arms, looked behind me, and shouted, *'Nein.'* As I turned to see what was going on, Rupert shot him dead with the Luger. Naturally I was astounded and chewed Rupert out. He looked at me as though I were crazy. He said, 'Why are you pissed off? Now it's a five-way split.' ''

''What happened then?''

''I said I wanted no part of it. Rupert said I could either keep my mouth shut and share in the treasure or get what he'd given the German. I saw nothing to my advantage in choosing the latter option. I informed Rupert I would not in any way profit from murder.''

''Good for you.''

''When I wrote the report I said the German resisted a demand for surrender by aiming the Luger at Rupert and that Rupert had no choice but to shoot him.''

''Professor, you disappoint me.''

''What choice did I have? Rupert had already killed one man. Not that I had any sympathy for a Nazi who was certainly destined to be hanged as a war criminal. Rupert merely hastened the date of Kadiddlehopper's certain execution.''

''I recall you saying something earlier today about the

pages of history being littered with dreary rationales for justifying winking at evil. And let's not talk of treasure. It was loot.''

Woolley shrugged. "Call it anything you wish.''

"The stuff didn't belong to that German officer. Whatever he had was still the property of the people he got it from. The four who took it from him compounded the crimes of the man they executed.''

Woolley looked at Nick incredulously. "Do you truly believe it could have been returned to its rightful owners?''

"Quite a lot of items pillaged by Nazis have been returned, if not to the original owners, to their heirs. If an effort could have been made in this instance, some of the loot could well have found its way back where it belonged.''

Woolley sighed. "One can not undo history, Nick.''

"What did the four do after Rupert shot the German?''

"They wrote out and signed four papers in which they agreed to split whatever they found, and swore themselves to secrecy. Each copy bore all their signatures.''

"Very smart of them. They each had an insurance policy.''

"They called it their compact.''

"Was there really a cache of loot?''

"Indeed so. Jewelry, loose gems, currency—U.S. dollars and British pounds, quite a lot of Swiss francs. It was buried and retrieved shortly after the war, before the Cold War really took hold and Russia slammed the Iron Curtain to divide Germany.''

"Do you know what happened after the four dug up the loot?''

"Despite the pledge of secrecy, Lazarus confided in me. He was always the weak link in the plot. He may have been a fool, but he was not without conscience. After the initial blush of wealth, he was troubled. He needed to talk about it, perhaps in the hope of finding justification. He knew I could be trusted, so he turned to me.''

"What did he tell you?''

"The loot was placed in a bank vault in London. Over a few years the currency was laundered, to use a term of today, and the jewels and other items were sold piece by piece, with the proceeds being parceled out among the four. But the crazy thing about all this was that the prize Rupert valued most was that Luger.''

"I can't believe you kept quiet all these years.''

"Whenever I experienced pangs of conscience I remembered the fate of Captain Kadiddlehopper. I enjoyed living, Nick.''

"How did they manage to handle getting rid of the loot?''

"Rupert took care of it. He used his reputation in the world of antiques dealers to dispose of jewelry and other valuables on yearly visits to London and the Continent. He made his last trip about five years ago. With the final disposal of proceeds, which took place in Lazarus's cottage, the partnership was to be dissolved and the four copies of the compact they'd signed torn up and burned. Ironically that was the weekend Gold drowned in a boating accident.''

"So instead of the last of the spoils being quartered,'' said Nick, "there was a three-way split.''

"Exactly.''

"Did it ever occur to you that Gold's accident was a very convenient turn of events?''

"Of course I wondered about it. But it wasn't my business.''

"I know what Rupert and Lazarus did after the last division of the loot. They returned to Cambridge. What did Little do?''

"Jonathan moved to London.''

"When was the last time you saw him?''

"Three years ago. I was visiting London and called on him. He was the head of a charitable committee sponsoring a concert that weekend at the Albert Hall. The following evening I treated Little to dinner at the Sherlock Holmes Pub. I haven't seen him since.''

"Does Little still live in London?''

"That is where I sent the telegram to apprise him of the memorial I've arranged for Rupert.''

"Why didn't you phone him?''

"I did. The person who answered said Little had been called away on Sunday, but did not say when to expect him back.''

"One more question, Professor. Why did you think after the Rupert murder that Lazarus might have been somehow involved?"

"On Sunday Lazarus had created a scene with Rupert at the Widener. When Rupert was killed on Monday night I thought the two events were related. My apprehension mounted when Lazarus went missing. But after I saw what happened to his apartment I began to think that Lazarus disappeared because he was afraid whoever killed Rupert would also come after him."

"Your alter-ego Jake Elwell would have seen that the mess that had been made of Lazarus's apartment was proof that Lazarus was not in danger. If someone wanted him dead, you'd have found Lazarus's corpse. Jake would have looked at that apartment and wondered what the man who trashed it was looking for. I think if Jake were with us now he'd have one more question for you."

"Since he is not with us," said Woolley, "I assume you are prepared to act on his behalf."

"I believe Jake would ask how you can be certain that at the last meeting, the four burned *all* copies of their compact?"

"Why wouldn't they detroy them? The compact's purpose was achieved. All the treasure, that is, the loot had been equally distributed."

"Agreeing to equal distribution was one purpose. But they had a second reason for making it. It was a mutual safeguard against any of the four revealing what they'd done. As I said, it was an insurance policy. It guaranteed none of the four could spill the beans without incriminating himself. It was also a kind of *life* insurance. If one died the beneficiaries divided the estate, as they did after Gold drowned."

"All very interesting, Nick, but there was little left of the treasure—sorry, loot. With the last of it divided and now with three of the four dead, whether one copy of the compact or all of them exist is moot."

"In view of the fact that there is no statute of limitations on murder, even when the victim was a Nazi war criminal, I doubt the fourth man would agree with you."

# Nineteen

WITH DUSK DESCENDING into night as they crossed the Charles from Boston to Cambridge on the Harvard Bridge, Nick shattered a silence that had filled the car like a winter fog since shortly after they left Barnstable. "You had a key to Lazarus's place," he said, jolting Woolley out of a half slumber. "Would you also happen to have one to Rupert's house?"

Rubbing his eyes, Woolley yawned. "I do indeed."

"I don't suppose you have it with you?"

Woolley dug into a pocket, produced a ring of keys, jingled them, and smiled slyly.

"That's good," Nick said. "I have a rule against breaking into more than one house per day."

"What will you be looking for?"

"I'll tell you when I find it. If I find it."

Ten minutes later he parked the car in front of Rupert's Victorian house. Gazing across a tidy lawn, Woolley said, "This is the first important thing Rupert bought after the war."

"The first division of spoils must have been substantial," Nick said, getting out of the car. "This house cost a pretty penny, even in postwar money."

When they stood in a large foyer, Woolley said, "I've never searched someone's home. Where do we begin?"

"When you're looking for secrets," Nick said as he

started up a staircase, "it's wise to begin in the bedroom."

Following Nick, Woolley suddenly giggled nervously.

Nick looked back at him sternly. "What's so amusing?"

"I'm sorry," Woolley whispered, "I had a flash of memory of the private detective going up steps in an old house like this in the movie *Psycho*."

Nick peered up the stairs. "Do you happen to know which of the bedrooms was Rupert's?"

"It's directly opposite the top of the stairs."

Finding a chair facing the open door, Nick said, "A curious spot to sit, wouldn't you say?" After examining the carpet around it, he looked at festooned walls. "You don't have to be Sherlock Holmes to deduce that the person who slept in here was in love with history. And with himself."

Woolley said, "*Si monumentum requiris circumspice*."

"If you would see the man's monument," said Nick as he moved slowly about the room, "look around."

"Bravo, Nick! I'm delighted to note you have not forgotten how to translate your schoolboy Latin."

"I always thought my apartment was a museum to one man's inflated ego."

As Nick studied a picture of four young men wearing World War II helmets and smoking cigars, Woolley reached around him and touched a fingertip to each face, left to right. "Lazarus, Gold, Rupert, Little. The place: outside Ohrdruf Nord camp in Germany on April 12, 1945. The very day President Roosevelt died, but we hadn't learned that at the time."

"Where were you when this was taken?"

Woolley lowered his hand and placed it lightly on Nick's shoulder. "I was the cameraman."

"Was this taken before or after Rupert shot the Nazi?"

"The day after. They had just found the . . . loot and come from reburying it."

"Had they written their compact by then?"

"That was done before they found the spot indicated on the map Kadiddlehopper gave me."

"They must have been confident of finding something. Whose idea was the mutually incriminating compact?"

"Jonathan Little suggested it."

Still looking at the photo, Nick said, "They certainly seem pleased with themselves. You'd think one of them had just learned he'd become a father and handed out cigars."

"The stogies were their way of celebrating the discovery of Kadiddlehopper's cache. It really was a treasure trove, Nick. A king's ransom."

Disgusted, Nick said, "It's people like them who give cigars a bad reptutation." Moving sideways, he pointed to the photo of the four, older and with water behind them. "Did you also snap this one?"

"That was taken on the sundeck of Lazarus's cottage, but not by me. There probably was no photographer as such. Lazarus owned one of those cameras with a timer."

As Nick moved slowly around the bedroom, Woolley asked, "Did you ever wear a uniform, Nick?"

"Policeman's blue."

"I meant a miltary uniform."

Examining titles of books on the shelves covering half the wallspace, Nick replied, "In the Second World War I was a child. When Korea broke out I was in high school. After I graduated in 1952 I had an exemption from the draft because I'd been accepted for the police academy. I fought the Vietnam War on the streets of New York and campuses of Columbia University and City College and by tangling with New York University antiwar protesters in clouds of marijuana smoke in Washington Square Park."

"Ah yes, the sixties and seventies. It seemed as if the tumult and shouting in Harvard Yard would never cease."

"Were you one of the tumulters and shouters?"

"Had I been on the Columbia University faculty," Woolley said with twinkling eyes, "you and I might have met under much different circumstances."

Nick smiled. "It would have been an honor to arrest you."

Woolley turned slightly and gazed through a window into the distance. "My war was simpler and cleaner. Or so I thought before I entered that cursed extermination camp." His eyes turned toward Nick. "If you had been there, you might not be quite so willing to condemn Rupert and the others—and me—as you are today.''

''I was born to be a cop, Professor. Murder is murder.''

Woolley's eyes shifted again to the picture of the warriors. ''We all were barely out of our teens at the time.''

''How old was the German Rupert shot?''

''A few years older, probably. He was a captain.''

''You were a lieutenant.''

''I did not slaughter innocents. As a matter of fact, none of us ever shot anyone in combat.''

''How did you and the others come to be interrogators?''

Woolley sat in the chair facing the door. ''We were graduates of an American public school system that, alas, no longer exists. In my time students planning on college had to take two foreign languages, not including Latin. Everyone had to study that, but I'm sure very few remember the mother of all tongues as well as you appear to. What foreign languages did you study?''

''I took Spanish and French,'' said Nick, opening a closet and finding suits. ''As a cop in New York, I had no need for parlaying bo-coo Fron-say, but after a while Spanish came in *mucho* handy.''

''When the army learned we all got straight As in German,'' Woolley said, remembering Nick's question, ''we were immediately classified linguists. We met in a staging area on the southeast coast of England shortly before the invasion of France.''

Nick shut the closet door. ''You went ashore on D-Day?''

''D-Day plus one.''

Standing in front of the showcase for Rupert's cigar-box collection, Nick looked at the cigar humidor on its top and the object next to it. Lifting the Luger by the barrel, he held it up to show Woolley. ''Does this have a familar look to you?''

Woolley stroked his beard. ''It's astonishing to me that he held on to that thing all these years.''

''Why not? It's a real beauty.'' Replacing the gun, Nick said, ''What's astonishing is that the police who inspected this room not only left it here, they didn't grasp its significance.''

Woolley pondered a moment, then snapped his fingers. ''I see what you mean. You'd expect to find a gun in a drawer or closet. This one is out in the open.''

Looking down at the pistol, Nick said, ''It's also loaded.'' Opening the humidor and finding it empty, he muttered, ''Rupert really was out of cigars.''

Bending over the humidor to inhale the aroma of cedar, he recalled his surprise on Monday morning at seeing Rupert awake so early to demand promised Montecristos that, if he stuck to his custom, wouldn't be touched before noon. Taking two boxes. Leaving the others in his locker. Claiming someone had gotten the better of him Sunday night. Complaining of slick forgers of the detritus of history and other things and then talking about a nonexistent Columbus diary on the subject of *cigarros*!

A clever trick to entice an ex-cop to his office!

Taking the key to his locker from his trousers pocket and disappearing in the walk-in humidor to store the four boxes of Montectristos. Coming out and asking ''When do you shut up your shop today, Nick?'' when he knew he closed at eight on Mondays.

''Then I shall expect you in my office,'' he said as he left the store, ''at eight-fifteen.''

Why not eight-ten? Eight-twenty? Half past eight?

Woolley's voice plucked Nick back to the present, speaking from an out-of-place chair. ''If Rupert had his Luger out it can only mean one thing. He felt he had to guard against something.''

Nick shut the humidor. ''Not something, Professor. Some*one*. Rupert's mistake was not recognizing the danger came from the person who smoked a Montecristo with him Monday night.''

Woolley rose slowly from the chair. ''What will you do now?''

Nick pocketed the Luger. ''Drop you at home.''

Less than an hour later, Nick entered Lerch's second-floor office. ''I figured you'd be burning the midnight oil.''

Painted an eerie chartreuse by the light from a green-shaded desk lamp, Lerch looked up from paperwork. "A detective's work is never done."

The black Luger clunked onto the desk.

"All right," said the detective, staring at the gun, "what's this that you've brought me like a proud house cat dragging home a dead field mouse?"

"It's a memento."

"Not yours," Lerch said as his eyes went from the pistol to Nick's face. "A Luger is not exactly police department issue."

"Like all such trophies it has a very interesting story."

"Swell," Lerch said, indicating that Nick should sit. "I have always loved a good yarn before bedtime."

Nick dug into a pocket for his cigar case, remembered where he was, and said, "I warn you, it's a horror story."

Lerch leaned back, folded hands behind his head, and smiled. "Goody-goody gumdrops."

As Nick's narrative flowed from Cambridge to Barnstable and back, the easy rocking of Lerch's chair alternately put Lerch in shadows and ghostly green light.

When the story was finished Lerch stopped moving, leaned across his desk, and gleefully exclaimed, "Nick, I haven't come across a more farfetched tale since I read—"

"Sir Arthur Conan Doyle?"

Stiff as a rifle barrel, Lerch looked puzzled. "I referred to Robert Louis Stevenson's *Treasure Island*."

"A good story," Nick said, "but it lacked one thing to make it perfect. A detective."

"If Rupert was afraid his life was in danger," Lerch said, thoughtfully stroking the pistol with a thick fingertip, "why would he leave the Luger at home?"

"Reading a dead man's mind has never been my strong suit."

Lerch's finger abandoned the pistol. "May I hazard an answer to my own question?"

"Certainly."

"Just because you found a gun in the bedroom," Lerch said, giving the pistol a tap of a fingertip, "is no reason to jump to the conclusion Rupert had it out because he was frightened. Maybe he always kept it where you found it. You said his bedroom looked like a museum. The thing was a war souvenir.''

''Every other memento in that room was displayed on a wall.''

''He could have taken it down to admire it. To clean it.''

''Who cleans a loaded gun?''

''Accepting your theory *for argument's sake* that Rupert had the gun handy because he was afraid of someone, you still have to explain why he didn't have the gun with him Monday night.''

''That he didn't *suggests* he felt frightened only when he was home alone. Remember the position of the chair in the bedroom. It had been turned to face the door.''

''You assume it had been turned that way.''

''The indentations in the carpeting support that assumption.''

''But you have no way of knowing when the chair was turned. I also point out that you did not find the Luger near the chair. It was across the room next to the humidor on top of the display case. If he was so much in fear why was it there?''

Nick mulled this over for a moment. ''I'd say he put it there because he assumed the danger had passed.''

''Come on, Nick! Doesn't that back my idea that he always kept it there? The threat he felt—or imagined—didn't materialize, so he returned the gun to its usual place next to the humidor. He probably was so glad nothing had happened he lit up a cigar in relief.''

''He couldn't have. The humidor was empty.''

''Because it was empty when you looked in it doesn't mean he hadn't one left. I say he did and smoked it.''

''I know for a fact there couldn't have been any in it. There were no ashes. No cigar band. No butt. Also, when he came to my store Monday morning he told me he had given away his last cigar Sunday evening. He took two boxes of Montecristos, one for his office, the other to stock the empty bedroom humidor when he got home Monday night. He stressed the word 'empty' as though he had discovered somebody had made off with his life's savings.''

Lerch folded his hands atop the paperwork. "If Woolley's yarn about a cache of Nazi loot was true those life's savings must have been substantial. Has the old saying, 'Where there is a will, there are relatves with a motive for murder,' ever entered your mind in this case?''

"It has now.''

Lerch tapped a finger to his temple. "It's been stuck in my head as though my brain was made of Velcro. I've had Gary Evert working that angle, but, alas, with no success.''

"I've never been keen on criticizing another copper,'' Nick said, getting up to leave, "but Evert also overlooked the Luger.''

Lerch's greenish face scowled. "That is a little matter I intend to discuss with the sergeant first thing in the morning.''

"I wouldn't be too hard on him,'' Nick said lightheartedly, going out the door. "He probably saw it and figured it was just one more meaningless item on display in Rupert's museum.''

# PART III

## Ashes to Ashes

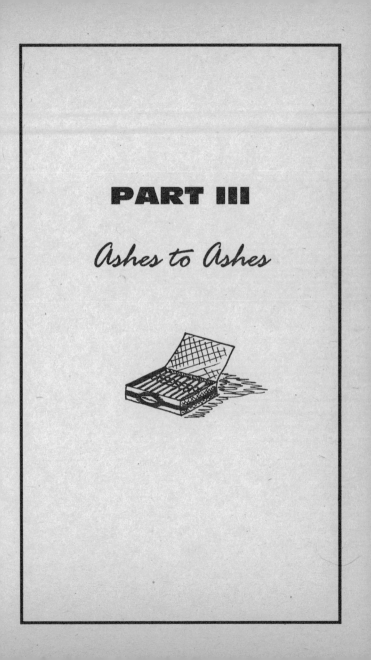

# Twenty

AS NICK AND Woolley approached Appleton Chapel on a sunny Tuesday afternoon one week and a day after Rupert's murder and Lazarus's suicide, Jack Lerch and Sergeant Evert stood in the doorway of Sever Hall.

"Look at them," said Woolley contemptuously. "They believe they're discreet, but they stick out like two broken thumbs. How can they not realize that everyone in the Yard recognizes them as cops trying not to look like cops?"

"Maybe they want everybody to recognize them," said Nick as they entered the chapel.

With its elegant white spire in the manner of the English architect Christopher Wren, the church afforded those who came to commemorate Stanley Rupert and Jerome Lazarus Corinthian columns and pilasters, heavy-muntined rounded windows, and a wineglass pulpit. Also in severe Colonial style, the rows of hard pews were chalk-white.

Taking a seat next to Nick at the front, Woolley turned halfway so as to see everyone who entered.

Nick whispered, "Now who's a broken thumb?"

"I have a reason to look at who is attending," said Woolley, indignantly. "I am the ringmaster."

"You make a memorial service sound like a circus."

"The only occasion that surpasses a memorial service in the show business department, in my view, is a funeral. I'm glad that both Rupert and Lazarus had the good sense to leave instructions that they be cremated. That's what I plan for myself. There will be no posturing at a circus such as this one about what a fine person I was, followed by a free lunch. I want nothing in the way of shallow ritual.''

A few moments later Nick felt the jab of an elbow.

"Coming down the aisle," Woolley said quietly, "is Rupert's family. The elderly woman is Rebecca Rupert, nee Henry, Stan's widow, if that term may be applied to a divorced wife. She did not remarry, which suggests something about her attitude toward marriage after her experience with Stan. The woman with her is the only child of that short-lived union. Her name is Millicent. Married name Trevellyan.''

"Attractive lady," said Nick.

"She's put on a few pounds since the last time I saw her. The young man is her son, Rex, as handsome as Stanley was in his twenties. They live on Beacon Hill in a house that's well beyond their means, but not Grandmother's. What a troika of suspects!''

With a glance at them as they settled in a middle pew Nick also spoke softly, "Why should any of them want Rupert dead?''

"My dear Nick, it's a rule in mystery writing that when a wealthy man has been murdered there are plenty of relatives who stand to benefit from the deceased's will. Once the antiques shop and other property can be liquidated, and any other bequests are taken care of, they should each walk away with between a quarter and a half million. Or more.''

Nick shook his head slowly. "Professor, how do you know all this stuff?''

"I'm Stanley's executor. Didn't I mention that fact?''

"No," Nick said, turning forward and facing the pulpit, "but you should have informed Lerch. He's had Evert looking for a will for a week.''

"Here we have the official academic delegation," Woolley said with a slightly disdainful tone as he looked toward the rear of the chapel.

Nick swung around.

"The leader is Robert Treat," Woolley continued. "Following him are Margo Palmer and James Philbrick. They are Stan's former academic colleagues. Please note that I have not described them as Stan's friends.''

The academics chose pews closer to the pulpit.

Presently Woolley stood to greet a frail-looking, gray-haired woman clutching a crumpled white handkerchief.

''Oh my dear,'' he said, stepping into the aisle to hug Sara Hobart. ''What a heartbreaking week this must have been for you.''

Her eyes turned to Nick. ''Hello, Mr. Chase.''

Woolley said, ''You two know one another?''

''Stan occasionally sent me to Nick's store to pick up cigars from his, uh, what do you call that little safelike box in that big glass room where Stan stored his cigars?''

''A humidor,'' said Nick. ''I'm sorry to see you again on such a sad occasion.''

She tenderly touched Nick's shoulder. ''Thank you for being Stan's friend.''

As she found a seat across the aisle, Woolley whispered to Nick, ''Sara Hobart is the embodiment of loyalty. She foolishly gave up more than thirty years catering to Stan Rupert's needs and whims.''

''Why foolishly?''

''How would you describe a woman who spent a lifetime in love with someone who was incapable of loving her back?''

A chubby man of middle years sat beside Hobart.

''That is George Dickson,'' Woolley said quietly. ''He is the former curator of the Hermann collection of fifteenth-century European art at the Gordon Museum. He was dismissed in disgrace after Stanley questioned the authenticity of three acquisitions a couple of years ago. You may have read about the controversy in the newspapers several years back.''

''It rings a bell,'' said Nick. ''It's damn forgiving of him, coming to a memorial for a man who got him fired.''

Woolley smiled slyly and faced forward. ''The last laugh is not always the loudest. Sometimes it's a chortle at the funeral. The beefy chap next to Dickinson is probably enjoying one now. Stuart Mosley is an historian. Stanley's review of an article in a learned journal a year ago did serious damage to Mosley's reputation. Stan accused him of plagiarism. And bad writing.''

"Is there anyone here Rupert didn't alienate?"

Woolley turned again toward the rear. "The tall gentleman with the silver-headed walking stick just coming in is Jonathan Little. I *know* you will want to talk with him about the case.''

"That's Jack Lerch's job."

Still looking to the back, Woolley watched Peg Baron enter. "My, my, Nick. Look who has arrived with your lady friend. Do you know who that man is?''

Nick watched Peg Baron and Wilhelm Wieder find a pew. "He plays the piano."

"*Plays* the piano? Wilhelm Wieder does not *play* the piano. He transforms it. I'm lucky to have gotten a pair of tickets for a recital he's giving at Boston Conservatory Saturday night. I'd expected to attend with Lazarus. Perhaps you'd care to go?''

"Saturday night? Sorry," Nick said, still looking at Peg. "Sam Gargan and I are going to a Bruins game."

"Here's an unexpected appearance," Woolley said, indicating another young man moving slowly down the aisle. "I wonder how he found out this event was being held."

"Who is he?"

"Rupert's nephew Harry. He's the son of Stan's late brother, who married late and died young. Hence the fact that Harry and Rex are roughly the same age.''

With no indication of others entering, Woolley stood facing the sparse audience.

"Because I am not a religious man," he said, "I shall not be a hyopcrite by taking to the pulpit to address you. Anyone who wishes to do so is, of course, welcome to it. In speaking of my lengthy friendship with Stanley Rupert and Jerome Lazarus I'll be brief. As Mark Anthony said as he stood over the body of Caesar, 'I am no orator.' ''

The last to leave the chapel, the elderly woman Woolley had identified as Rupert's former wife paused on the steps, left her grandson, and approached Woolley to place a light kiss on his left cheek. "Roger. You are still an incorrigible fibber."

"My dear Rebecca, I haven't the faintest idea what you are talking about."

"I refer to that deceptive remark about not being an orator. Your tributes to Stanley and Jerome were simply inspired. You hit all the right chords."

"You are very kind. I'm so glad you were able to be here, and I'm sure that if Stanley could know that you came he would be very pleased."

"You know as well as I that if Stan were able to see me here he would assume I came to satisfy myself that he was truly dead." With a half smile at Nick, she asked, "And who is this?"

Woolley introduced Nick, who gave a slight nod and said, "You have my condolences."

"You were a friend of Stan?"

"I shared his passion for fine cigars."

The woman's eyes shifted toward her grandson and found Rex in animated conversation with Sara Hobart. "So does Rex. It must be an inherited masculine trait."

Observing Rex, Nick said, "Speaking of cigars, I have four boxes of them belonging to Stan."

Woolley said, "Nick is a tobacconist."

"Since Professor Woolley will be dispensing the things that make up your late husband's estate, I can turn them over to him to pass on to Rex."

"I've been trying to persuade him to quit smoking. But I'll tell him about the cigars. Or perhaps Stanley's nephew would be interested in them. Smoking has always been one of Harry Rupert's vices, though certainly not the worst of them."

As Sara seemed to abruptly end her conversation with Rex and hurry away, Nick heard the booming of a man's voice from behind. "Woolley, you're a born preacher!" Throwing arms around Woolley in a bear hug, Jonathan Little continued, "It has been too long between meetings. When was the last time?"

Woolley thought a moment. "The Albert Hall concert,

dinner the next evening at the Sherlock Holmes Pub. Three years ago?''

"I was surprised to see Wilhelm Wieder here today."

"He's a friend of a woman who is a friend of the man beside me. This is Nick Chase. He may want to question you."

Little greeted Nick with a slight nod. "Do the police consider me a suspect, Mr. Chase?"

"I'm not with the police, but I'm curious as to why you'd think they'd suspect a man who lives in London?"

"At the time of the murder I wasn't in London. I was here."

Woolley exclaimed, "Why you didn't you tell me?"

"Well, I never got to Cambridge, actually. When I said I was here I meant Boston. I never went beyond the Parker House Hotel. But I never expected it was Rupert who was in trouble. Judging by the state Lazarus was in when he phoned me I assumed it was he."

Nick asked, "When did Lazarus call you?"

"Sunday a week ago. It was late in London, so it had to have been afternoon here."

"You said he was in a state. What do you mean?"

"Lazarus's nerves were always on edge. But I had never known him to be as frantic as on that occasion. He insisted I get on the next plane to Logan Airport."

"Did he explain why?"

"He said he didn't dare tell me on the telephone. I booked a seat on the first flight out the next day."

"Arriving at what time?"

"I got in at five Monday afternoon. I arrived at the Parker House about an hour later and telephoned Lazarus. However, he did not answer. I kept trying till around eleven o'clock, then gave up and went to bed. When I read of Rupert's death in the paper Tuesday morning I grabbed the next plane back to London."

"I must say, Mr. Little, I find that astonishing. You knew an old friend had been murdered, you had failed to contact another old friend whose alarming phone call brought you dashing across the Atlantic, and you *went home*? If the police do talk to you they are likely to want to know why."

"I had history's oldest reason for running away, Mr. Chase. Fear. After I was unable to speak to Lazarus and then learned of Rupert's murder I was too terrified to stay."

"Yet a week later you're back, apparently unafraid."

Before Little could reply, Woolley interjected, "If you don't want to talk to police now, Jonathan, you'd better leave, because here they come."

A moment later Lerch and Evert arrived at the chapel and approached Chase and Woolley.

Lerch's eyes explored Little. "And who are you, sir?"

"According to Mr. Chase, I'm someone who might be of help in your inquiry."

Lerch smiled. "No time like the present."

"Fine. But I want Mr. Chase and Woolley present."

Watching Peg Baron leave the chapel arm in arm with Wieder, Nick said, "There's a good restaurant nearby. Farley's. It has a cigar room. I suggest we discuss this there."

Exiting Harvard Yard to Peabody Square, they skirted the Common where Washington had taken command of the Continental Army under an elm tree, walked half a block on Waterhouse Street, and arrived at a red brick building signified as a restaurant only by a brass plaque with its name. Upstairs a room carefully crafted to evoke the atmosphere of a men's private club was all maroon leather, dark woods, dim lights, and a gossamer haze of tobacco smoke suffused by aromas of superior spiritous drinks. The moment after they were seated in a corner banquette H. Upmann Lonsdales appeared at each place, along with matches and clippers.

"With my compliments, gentlemen," Nick said.

"An excellent selection, Mr. Chase," said Little, removing the band. "You are a man who knows cigars."

Woolley said, "I thought you knew, Johnathan. Nick owns the best cigar store in New England."

"How exciting," Little said, ignoring the clipper and taking a punch from a pocket. "Now that cigars seem to have become the rage everywhere you must be doing very well, Mr. Chase."

"Everyone calls me Nick."

"Excuse me," said a waiter. "Something from the bar?"

Following a personal rule against drinking alcohol on duty, Lerch ordered cranberry juice for himself. Evert asked for Diet Coke. Woolley and Little preferred beer. Without having to ask Nick was served Bushmills Irish whiskey neat in a fluted glass. Lifting it in a toast, he said, "To all the good things of life, starting with cigars."

Lerch ignored his juice. "Just so everything is straight at the outset, Mr. Little—"

"Jonathan, please."

"I've heard the story of the Nazi and the so-called treasure that is the link between you, Woolley, Rupert, Lazarus, and the fourth man who drowned a few years ago," Lerch continued. "I know about the division of the spoils of war, and the four copies of the compact you all burned in Lazarus's house at Barnstable."

"I appreciate your forthrightness," said Little, opening the end of his cigar with the punch. "However, I must correct you on one point. All copies of the compact were not burned."

Woolley slapped the table, rattling the silverware. "This is news to me! Lazarus led me to believe otherwise."

"After Gold drowned," Little said, laying down his cigar as a waiter handed everyone menus, "I refused to go through with the plan."

Nick spoke on a gust of cigar smoke. "In view of the fact the whereabouts of Gold's copy of the compact were unknown, you were wise not to." He paused while another waiter took one order for fish for Lerch and three for steak and potatoes. "Which of you insisted you proceed with the burning?"

Little gazed at his drink as if he were studying it. "I'm afraid this puts me in the rather awkward position of speaking ill of the dead."

Woolley said, "The dead can't hear you, Jonathan."

"Rupert was so adamant about going on with the plan and so furious with me for refusing he flung his in the fire anyway."

Lerch asked, "What did Lazarus do with his copy?"

"He was always intimidated by Rupert. He threw his in also."

"So as far as you knew," Nick said, "yours was the only copy of the compact left."

Little nodded. "Correct."

"Where is your copy at this moment?"

Little glanced furtively at Woolley.

"Everything has to come out," Woolley said. "Tell them."

Little sighed. "This will sound ghoulish, but you must keep in mind that we were very young." Pausing, he sipped his beer. "I keep it in a drawer in an old King Edward cigar box with another item from that day. Each of us took something from the body. For me it was the double lightning insignia of the SS the officer had on his collar. Lazarus claimed his dagger. Gold helped himself to a belt buckle."

Nick said, "Rupert took his Luger."

"He also took his identity papers."

Lerch looked at Woolley with disgust. "What memento did you take, Professor?"

Little answered heatedly. "He played no part in any of what the four of us did."

"That's not true," Nick said, looking into Woolley's eyes. "He covered it up."

Lerch sipped cranberry juice. "All this is just fascinating, but I don't see how GIs picking the pockets of a dead Nazi more than fifty years ago is at all relevant to a murder in Cambridge, Massachusetts, eight days ago."

"How can you ignore the fact," Woolley demanded, "that out of five of us who were together on that day, three have had their lives ended violently?"

"Professor, I'm sure you are a very good mystery writer," said Sergeant Evert, "but if you are suggesting those deaths were the work of one of the five the logical suspects would be Little and yourself. Since he was on his way to London when Lazarus was in Barnstable, by process of elimination that leaves you."

"That is utter nonsense and you know it."

"Of course it's nonsense. That's why your idea that Gold's drowning, Rupert being murdered, and Lazarus hanging himself are somehow related to what happened in Germany is also nonsense.''

"All I know," Woolley said, "is that the day after Lazarus telephoned Jonathan in London in a state of obvious alarm, Rupert was murdered, and a couple of days later Lazarus was dead.''

With a puzzled expression Lerch looked up from his juice. "What's this about Lazarus making a phone call?''

"That phone call, Jack," said Nick, "is why we're here.''

Lerch's cheeks turned angry red. "Then why the devil have we been beating around the bush with this stuff that happened in World War II? Or am I to believe that after all this time the ghost of that dead Nazi decided to seek revenge?''

Little's face went pale. "What a chilling coincidence that you would speak of the very thing Lazarus ranted about during his phone call. He told me Rupert insisted he had seen just that.''

Exasperated, Lerch asked, "Just that . . . *what*?''

"There'd been a meeting between Lazarus and Rupert on Sunday afternoon during which, according to Lazarus, Rupert claimed that he thought he saw a ghost that noon in Harvard Square.''

Had Roger Woolley been a cartoon character, Nick thought as Woolley looked at him, a light bulb would have been drawn over his head. "That's why he looked as if he was having a coronary.''

Lerch banged down his fork. "For the record, gentlemen, the Cambridge Police Department does not believe in ghosts. Now, will somebody at this table please plant his feet firmly on the floor and start making sense?''

"I'll give it the old college try," said Nick. "After lunch on Sunday as Rupert and Professor Woolley were crossing Harvard Square, Rupert appeared to Woolley to have taken ill. Rupert said it was an upset stomach. Obviously, he'd seen something that left him so disturbed that he sat up all night in his bedroom with his chair turned toward the door with a gun at the ready. That means the danger he was confronting was flesh and blood.''

Woolley slapped the table. "Of course it does!"

"I can only tell you," said Little, "that Lazarus was quite frantic. Distraught. Scared. He mentioned Rupert's having seen a ghost and then begged me to come to Cambridge immediately. But when I arrived I was unable to contact Lazarus."

Lerch asked, "Did you contact Rupert?"

"I thought it better to see Lazarus first. If you doubt me, Mr. Lerch, you can verify all this with the people at the Parker House. I was in my room until I checked out on Tuesday morning."

"You knew Rupert very well," Lerch said. "Ghosts aside, who do you think might have killed him, and why?"

"I'm not an expert on murder. My field is antiques. That's why after the four of us had our last meeting I moved to London and opened a dealership in Curzon Street."

Nick said, "Once upon a time I was considered something of an expert on murder, and even now I find myself thinking like a detective. I naturally look at what I'm told to believe with a wary eye, which is why I don't buy your explanation for your move to London."

"I'm sorry, Nick, I don't follow you."

"I think you left the country following that meeting because you suspected Gold's death was not an accident, and that Rupert possessed Gold's copy of the compact. You feared you might meet Gold's fate. That's why you refused to destroy your copy of the compact. It was still a life insurance policy. It's also why you moved to London. You could have gone into antiques here."

"Now I'm lost," said Lerch. "Why would Rupert kill Gold?"

Nick replied, "One third is always better than a fourth."

"If Rupert wanted more," Lerch said, "he could have gotten it all by killing Gold, Lazarus, and Mr. Little years sooner. Kill all, have all."

"Deaths one at a time early on were too risky. One so late in the game was unlikely to cause alarm, especially when the others *believed* all but the final portion of the loot had been split up. But you didn't believe it, did you, Jonathan? How long had you supected Rupert of not being on the level? That's why you refused to burn your copy of the compact, even after Rupert and Lazarus tossed theirs on the fire. It was your hold over Rupert.''

"This is guesswork, Nick.''

"Speculation, yes. There's no way to prove it. But I'm an old ex-cop who believes in circumstantial evidence. I think the weight of it in this sorry affair is virtually overwhelming.''

Delivered food was ignored, along with drinks and cigars as the four men sat in stunned silence. At last, Woolley whispered, "This moment is known in the theater as a pregnant pause. In my genre, the mystery novel, it's called a twist. You are handling the device superbly, Nick.''

"But not so cleverly as to have caught you by surprise I'm sure, my friend.''

Woolley stroked his beard and beamed. "You flatter me.''

Lerch groaned. "For crying out loud, Nick, get on with it.''

"To do so I have to go back to the murder of the Nazi.''

Lerch grabbed his cranberry juice. "I was afraid of that.''

"It's been my experience that nothing illuminates character as much as what people do in a crisis. It's then that qualities both admirable and despicable emerge: the men on *Titanic* who saw that women and children got into lifeboats first, contrasted with a crewman who was said to have disguised himself as a woman so as to get into a boat. On that day in Germany fifty years ago it was not, I regret to say, Woolley who grabbed that Nazi's pistol. It was Rupert. Had Woolley gotten the Luger we would not be sitting here today.''

Woolley nodded his head. "Thank you.''

"The moment Woolley found the map of where the loot would be found, Rupert not only executed the German, he delivered a very powerful signal to the others concerning who was now in command. It was a role he played from then on. He proposed the compact. He took charge of stashing the loot in London and used his cover as an antiques dealer to dispose of it. And when he kept control of every aspect. He alone knew what the loot was worth, and therefore how much of it was to be split with the other three. I think I'm safe in assuming that at no time did division of the spoils ever approach equality. The term coined by gangsters and casinos in Las Vegas for the practice is 'skimming.' Perhaps Gold suspected Rupert and confronted him.''

Lerch nodded. "And paid for that mistake with his life.''

"There's no way of knowing, of course,'' Little said, picking up his cigar. Finding it cold, he reached for some matches.

Nick pulled his cigar case from a pocket. "Take a fresh one. There's nothing as awful as smoking a cigar that's been relit.''

"May I point out, Nick,'' said Sergeant Evert, "that none of this has gotten us any closer to finding out who killed Rupert.''

"On the contrary,'' Nick said. "There's been considerable progress made here today, Sergeant.''

"Well, it's happened without me noticing it.''

"Until today there was the possibility that Lazarus killed Rupert and hanged himself in a fit of conscience. But we now know Lazarus phoned Jonathan in London to express such concern about Rupert that he begged Jonathan to come to Cambridge. Why would he do that if he intended to kill Rupert? And I doubt that Jonathan suddenly decided that since he was coming over here that he might as well kill Rupert. As to Professor Woolley, I know he couldn't have done it because he was in his apartment working on his book. I heard him typing when I returned to Brattle Street. Therefore, we've eliminated three suspects.''

# Twenty-one

"JONATHAN, IF YOU'D like to see Nick's store," said Woolley as they left the restaurant, "it's only a few blocks away."

"Another time," Little said. "I promised Rebecca, Millie, and Rex that I'd stop by their house on Beacon Hill."

Buttoning his topcoat, Lerch said, "My car's nearby. I'll be happy to give you a lift."

"Thanks, but I have to make a stop on the way. I'll take a taxi over to Boston."

As Little, Lerch, and Evert walked away, Woolley stood on the curb and cleared the ashes from his new pipe by tapping the bowl in his palm. When the men were out of hearing he addressed Nick sharply. "It was naughty and rude of you to have considered me a suspect. But gallant of you to clear me."

"As to that, I trust I haven't left myself out on a limb."

Woolley dropped the ashes in the gutter. "How so?"

"I told Lerch that you were in your apartment at the time of Rupert's murder, even though I don't know that for a fact."

"Of course I was there," Woolley said as they walked in the direction of Brattle Street. "You heard me at work writing."

"I heard typing sounds."

"Typing *equals* writing!"

"Professor, I've been on to your trick with a tape recorder since I first spotted it on your writing desk. You have a tape of your typing that you play to make it appear you are at work when you are taking a nap or otherwise goofing off, or you don't want me barging in on you."

"No wonder you are so good at crime detection, Nick. What a fantastic imagination you possess!"

"I've been listening to you at work for more than fifteen years. When you are actually beating that old upright machine to death, I can feel vibrations in my walls that I do not notice when you play the tape. When I went out that Monday night I heard the tape. When I came back you were really typing."

"I'd put the tape on because I did not want to be disturbed while I had a visitor."

Nick took a cigar from his case. "Who did you think might disturb you?"

"You have a habit of dropping in after you close the store."

"You knew I had an appointment that night with Rupert."

"There was every reason to believe you'd look in first. Your concern for the old man who lives upstairs is one of your most endearing qualities. But that evening I wanted no such intrusion, so I put on the tape of the typewriter."

Nick clipped the cigar and smiled. "I see. Did your mystery visitor happen to be . . . a lady?"

"How droll, Nick. The visitor was Jerome Lazarus."

Nick came to an abrupt stop and mouthed the unlit cigar. "I can't believe what you're saying! Why in hell didn't you inform Lerch of this immediately? You'd have cleared Lazarus."

"I said nothing because I was not certain Lazarus had not killed Rupert."

"If Lazarus was with you," Nick said, resuming walking, "he couldn't have done it."

"He was there when you left the store at eight o'clock, but he only knocked on my apartment door at a quarter before eight. That, as we were to learn, was well within the time frame in which the murder occurred."

"Why didn't you tell me this when I broke the news of the murder to you at six in the morning?"

"I felt I ought to speak to Lazarus first."

Nick removed the cigar and shook it at Woolley. "This isn't adding up, Professor. If you felt you ought to talk to Lazarus, why did you wait until two hours later to go look for him? Why didn't you phone him?"

"I tried. He didn't answer. We now know why. He'd left for the Cape by then."

"This gets more bizarre. You knew of Rupert's murder, yet you never considered he pulled his sudden disappearance because he *did* it?"

"I certainly thought that intially. But the evidence did not point conclusively in that direction. In light of all that had transpired I was not sure what to think. Before going to the police I needed some indication of what was true and what was not. You know the rest."

"Oh do I! You figured you could get an indication of the truth by dragging me into all this!"

"You were already in it, thanks to Rupert."

Nick stopped to perform the ritual of lighting the cigar, then declared, "You may not have broken the commandment against murder, my friend, but you sure trampled another."

"Which one would that be?"

"Thou shalt not lie. From the very beginning of this case you've done nothing but bear false witness. You've been a veritable fountain of deceit, prevarication, and chicanery."

"All in a worthy cause."

Walking again, Nick asked, "Am I right in deducing that you have also engaged in one instance of lawlessness not covered by the Tablets of Sinai? Breaking and entering!"

"I assume you refer to Lazarus's apartment."

Nick blew a column of smoke. "I certainly do. The mysterious ransacker was you. It was a way to bolster the proposition that Lazarus was in fear of his life, and to make sure I was hooked."

Reaching Brattle Street, Woolley smiled sheepishly. "That might have been a touch over the top melodramatically."

Peering ahead and assuring himself the Indian remained where it belonged, Nick said, "A *touch*?"

"You must admit that all the progress in this case has been your doing."

"What progress? It seems to me the case hasn't budged."

"You said in the restaurant that three suspects and a motive had been eliminated."

"I was referring to this dead-Nazi/loot/compact craziness. I never considered any of that particularly relevant. If any of the conspirators, including yourself, had reason to kill Rupert he'd have been found dead years ago, but probably not in his store. He'd have drowned like Gold."

"Excuse me, Nick," Woolley said as they reached The Happy Smoking Ground, "but I feel I must take umbrage at your reference to me as a conspirator. That is a groundless charge."

" 'The only thing necessary for the triumph of evil is for good men to do nothing,' someone once said."

"Edmund Burke."

Nick opened the white door. "Is that who it was? I thought it might have been Inspector Elwell."

Woolley blared a laugh. "As a matter of fact, Nick, he did say something like that in *Who Killed Alma Mater?*"

Holding the door open, Nick said, "By the way, Professor. Why *did* Lazarus come to see you that night?"

Woolley stroked his beard. "Didn't I say?"

Nick sighed in dismay. "No, you didn't."

"He'd been told that his cancer had metasticized."

"Lazarus had *cancer*?"

"Gotten into the brain. No hope whatever. Two, maybe three months left. That's what he wanted to tell Rupert at the Widener, and did tell him when they met Sunday afternoon. The poor man was desperately looking for somebody to agree to assist him, when he was ready, in having a dignified death. Rupert refused. I suppose that was the true purpose of his call to Jonathan Little. I know it's why he came to me. I told him I'd look into ways to do it. I presume he chose not to wait and went down to the Cape."

"If you knew this, why did you insist that Ludlum treat the death as a murder?"

"That was naughty of me, but I was afraid you might decide that Lazarus killed himself because he murdered Rupert. I didn't want you dropping the case."

Nick exploded with anger and a cloud of cigar smoke. "This isn't one of your books. This is a real murder case in which you have done nothing but withhold crucial information."

"What you need at the moment, Nick, is a little time to cool off," Woolley declared as he opened the door to the stairway to the apartments. "We'll talk again later."

Fuming as he entered the store, Nick found Sam Gargan at the counter reading a book. Looking up, Sam said, "Your lady was on the horn a couple of times. The last one, she said when you got back you're supposed to call her at home."

"Other than taking messages and reading books," Nick said as he strode behind the counter, "have you accomplished anything to justify your presence on these premises today?"

Sam straightened. "Offhand I'd estimate I did about eight hundred bucks' worth of justifying my presence. What's got you in a bad mood?"

"None of your business," Nick replied, picking up the phone.

Sam stepped aside. "I'll be in the humidor checking stock."

"When you're done bring me out a box of my Upmanns."

A voice on the phone answered, "Homicide. Sergeant Evert."

"Good, you're back from lunch. Is Lerch there?"

"He's down the hall . . . in the men's room. Can I help you, Nick?"

"Tell him to call me at my store ASAP."

A moment later, when Peg Baron heard Nick's voice, she asked, "Are any of the Boston teams playing at home this evening?"

''Not that I'm aware of.''

''Good. I'm redeeming my raincheck.''

''What raincheck?''

''The one you owe me for not being available to meet me at Farley's after the Tchaikovsky concert last week. This time I'm accepting no excuses.''

''I'll join you only when I hear you promise not to drag the piano player along.''

''Wilhelm happens to be dining with his brother. Nick, you wouldn't be feeling just a tad jealous?''

''Where'd you get that zany notion?''

''When you saw Wilhelm with me at the memorial service you made a point of avoiding me.''

''Baloney. When you came out of the chapel arm in arm with the piano player you avoided me.''

''I would have stopped to speak to you, but you were involved with Lerch, his assistant, Woolley, and somebody else. You all looked so damn serious. I assume you were discussing the case. You can tell me all the latest at Farley's. Six o'clock?''

''That's fine.''

As Nick hung up, Sam emerged from the walk-in humidor with a box of fifty Upmanns. ''Your stash is down to two boxes.''

''I've got more on order,'' Nick said. When the phone rang he answered it with ''Happy Smoking Ground.''

Lerch replied, ''Well, this is unhappy homicide. What's up?''

''You can scratch Jerome Lazarus from your list of suspects. It wasn't a guilty conscience that drove him to hang himself. It was apparently the big C. But considering my source for this bit of information, I suggest you confirm it with an autopsy.''

*Twenty-two*

"THE PART ABOUT the four men and the compact is thrilling," Peg said as a white-jacketed busboy cleared the table of dinner plates. "Now I know how Sam Spade's secretary felt when Sam told her about the Maltese falcon. But what a triple whammy for poor old Lazarus. He finds out he's got weeks to live, his oldest and closest friend refuses to assist him in cashing in his chips when the time comes, and then he learns that same friend has had his throat slit ear to ear. No wonder he strung himself up."

"You have such a colorful way of putting things, Peg. Have you ever considered giving up the cello and writing hardboiled detective novels?"

"And compete with Woolley? No thanks. But what a deliciously clever rascal he's turned out to be!"

"I wouldn't call obstruction of justice deliciously clever."

"No prosecutor in his right mind would dare to bring such a charge against that sweet old codger."

Nick took out his cigar case. "In addition to misleading the police that sweet old codger covered up a cold-blooded murder for over half a century."

"The man was a war criminal."

"He was a disarmed prisoner, and as officer in charge, Woolley had a duty to see him treated humanely under the rules of war."

" 'Humanely under the rules of war'? There's an oxymoron.''

"Let's not play word games, Peg. I have had enough of that with Woolley.''

"In a circumstance where Woolley's own life was at stake, I think he did the only reasonable thing. Rupert did have a pistol pointed at him.''

"There was no Luger pointing at Woolley when he wrote out a falsified report.''

"Nonetheless, Rupert still had it, and Woolley understood what that meant. He told you so himself. How long do suppose he would have survived if he tried to tell the truth? And if he had, it would have been his word against the word of the others. Do you truly believe anyone would have cared about how one more Nazi wound up dead? Especially one who had been an officer in a concentration camp? If Woolley was wrong a higher power than us will judge him for it.''

Nick chuckled. "Woolley does not recognize the existence of any power higher than a fiction editor.''

"Since you've shown that Rupert's murder could not have been related to the episode during the war, where does that leave the investigation?''

"Where it's belonged from the start. In Jack Lerch's lap.''

"You can't just walk away from this.''

"No? Just watch me.''

A waiter appeared beside the table. "Will you have coffee? Something from the dessert trolley perhaps?''

Peg replied, "Two coffees. No dessert for either of us.''

As the waiter withdrew, Nick jibed, "What gives you the right to decide whether I'll have dessert?''

"It's my way of atonement for your sin.''

"What sin?''

"Woolley covered up a murder. Nick Chase is prepared to walk away and let another go unsolved.''

"The two are not at all comparable.''

"In my opinion you're both guilty of one of the worst sins of all: *indifference*.''

Nick bristled. "I am not employed by the Cambridge

police to solve murders. My job is peddling tobacco.''

Peg smiled. ''Some people might say that's also a sin.''

''Oh brother! Has Peg Baron, stalwart liberal, lifelong Democrat, and defender of individual rights now enlisted in the antismoking gestapo?''

''If I minded smoking I would not be redeeming my raincheck from last week by paying for your dinner in the upstairs cigar room at Farley's.''

''The treat's on you? How very nice,'' Nick said, smiling as he loosened some buttons on his sweater.

Peg reached across the table and poked his belly. ''That is why you're not being allowed dessert.''

Nick held up his cigar and gazed at it admiringly. ''Thanks be to God these aren't fattening.''

''If they were,'' Peg said as the waiter brought two cups of black coffee, ''you'd weigh at least a ton.''

Nick struck a match and held the flame under the end of the Upmann. ''That is true,'' he said as the cigar went into his mouth, ''and I'd be a happier old fat man than Kasper Gutman would have been if the Maltese falcon had turned out to be genuine. Since you're obviously a fan of that movie, you might like to know that the brand of cigar Gutman gave Sam was a double Corona del Ritz. The booze they drank was Johnnie Walker Red. I have a bottle of it, if you'll permit me to redeem the raincheck for a nightcap that you handed me the night we had dinner with the piano player. How is the kid prodigy, by the way?''

''He's not a kid. Wilhelm Wieder is quite a sophisticated man of the world. You might appeciate that if you would quit being so damn hostile to him.''

Nick jerked the cigar from his mouth. ''When was I hostile?''

''Today at the memorial.''

''That was a surprise. I couldn't figure out why he was there.''

''Since he met you at the Union Oyster House he's been fascinated by the Rupert case and positively enthralled by you.''

Nick took a puff and blew smoke through a mischievous

smile. "Really? Is this sophisticated man of the world also gay?"

Peg's eyes narrowed to angry slits. "That is exactly what I meant about you being hostile."

"Peg, I was joking."

"I am not amused."

"Okay, I'm sorry. I'll change the subject."

"You're good at that."

"I thought this was supposed to be kiss-and-make-up time."

"So did I."

"Well, what the hell went wrong?"

"If you don't know, you'll never understand."

"How can anything not known be understood?"

Peg's eyes searched the room for their waiter. Catching his attention and pantomiming signing the check, she said, "I think we should have that Johnnie Walker nightcap after you've finished your investigation of the case."

"I am not investigating any case."

Presented with the bill, Peg opened her purse, took out a wallet, and removed a credit card. "Don't be silly. Of course you are."

Nick grabbed the check. "I'm a member here. I'll pay for the meal." After signing it, he pushed back from the table angrily. "Shall we go?"

"I think you should stay and finish your cigar," Peg said, leaving. "I'll take a cab home."

After waiting in hope that she would come back, Nick left the table, joined a crowd standing at the room's long mahogany bar, and felt a tap on his shoulder. Expecting Peg as he turned, he faced Dick Levitan.

"If you're planning to throw away any more good women, Nick, please let me know in advance."

Nick gazed at the exit. "I'm not positive, but I think she tossed me."

"Whatever the lady thinks your crime was, I'm sure she'll let you ask her to forgive you. Meantime, name your poison. I'll charge it to my expense account and you can tell me all the inside stuff you know about the murder of the antiques dealer."

Turning again to the bar, Nick said, "Johnnie Walker Red."

Levitan signaled the bartender.

"Where did you get the loony idea," Nick said, "that I know inside stuff?"

"J-W Red for my friend on my tab," Levitan said to the bartender. "It's not true that I know you know something," he said to Nick. "I'm guessing that the guy who found the body would know *something* newsworthy."

"Since when has Richard Levitan become a newsman?"

Levitan watched the drinks being poured. "I haven't. Being an all-night deejay pays better. But that does not mean I can't be as nosey as the newsies."

Nick took a sip of scotch. "You'll have to read the papers, or else ask Jack Lerch."

"I've been knocking around the Boston area all my life," Levitan said, ignoring his drink, "and I have learned you can't believe half of what they print and not a word that comes from Jack the Nimble, until he's ready to hold a news conference."

"That's very smart of him."

"I grant you Lerch is smart, which is why I'm puzzled that he hasn't cracked this case yet."

"I'm confident he will."

"Is that just the opinion of an ex-detective being loyal to a fellow cop, or am I right that you are closer to the investigation than you're willing to let on?"

"My only connection to the Rupert murder is that I was the person who found the body."

"Excuse me, Nick, but I find that as impossible to accept as Sherlock Holmes saying he didn't notice a damn thing."

Nick finished his scotch in a gulp. "Thanks for the drink, Dick. Have a good broadcast tonight. I'd tune in, but you're on the air well past my bedtime."

Levitan held Nick's arm. "One more question."

"If it's about the Rupert case you're wasting your breath."

"Of that I have an endless supply. I'm done with questions about the Rupert murder."

"Then what do you want to know?"

"Why don't you admit you're in love with Peg Baron, bite the bullet, and marry her?"

"Good night, Richard."

Levitan lifted his scotch in salute. "Good night, Nicholas. While the night people of Greater Boston are listening to me may you enjoy sweet dreams."

Outside the restaurant Nick stood smoking in a light misty rain and gazed across Waterhouse Street at the lamplight on budding trees of the Common where criminals had hanged before George Washington and Light Horse Harry Lee arrived to hammer rebellious Colonials into a neophyte American army. One hundred seventy years later their descendants mingled with sons and grandsons of immigrants to make war against a tyranny far worse than that of the king of the Britons. In that cause five young men named Woolley, Rupert, Lazarus, Little, and Gold, with a flair for the language of their enemy, met in a staging area on England's southeast coast, crossed the Channel, fought through France's fields and hedgerows, and invaded Germany with no way of foreseeing that in going over the river their battle maps called the Rhine, each crossed a personal Rubicon. In the cause of liberation they found themselves tangled in a wilderness of greed, betrayal, murder, suspicion, distrust, and deception for the remainder of their lives.

Walking slowly along Waterhouse Street in increasingly heavy rain, Nick came to its dead end at Garden Street. A left turn and then a right took him to Mason Street and Peg Baron's alma mater. Passing the graceful Georgian-inspired architecture of Radcliffe College, he tried to imagine her a Cliffie, as the rich Harvard hockey player delighted in calling his doomed working-class girlfriend in *Love Story*.

As he paused to take a final draw on his Upmann, he looked across Mason Street at lights in windows and tried to picture Peg taking down lecture notes in her impossible scrawl, poring over a book in her room while cramming for an exam, and dancing in the arms of the Harvard man she eventually married, of whom Nick knew no more than the fact he had been killed in Vietnam and buried in a military ceremony for a hero of a war the nation of Washington and Light Horse Harry Lee had abandoned.

Another left and a soaking stroll along James Street brought him to Brattle, three blocks from a store still being faithfully guarded by a figure clutching a bundle of wooden cigars. Lights in the third-floor windows indicated that advancement was being made in Jake Elwell's current murder investigation. The muted thumping sounds of typing through the walls of the apartment below added credence to the assumption.

A glowing red light of his answering machine signified that while dinner with Peg was being ruined at least one person had a reason to want to talk to him. The calls indicator registered 4. Mindful that Sam Gargan had been after him to replace the device with a digital recorder capable of registering not only how many calls had been recorded, but time and originating phone numbers, he rewound the message tape, hoping one of the four was Peg, and hit the Play button.

*Uh, Nick, ah, Mr. Chase, this is Sara Hobart, Stanley Rupert's assistant. Sorry to call you at home, but you were not at your store when I called there, so I looked you up in the book. I have something to tell you that might be important concerning Stan's murder. I'll try reaching you at your store tomorrow. Bye.*

After the message-is-ended beep, the tape continued:

*Hi, Dad, it's Jean. It's short notice, but Mike and I want to take you to dinner Saturday night. We're dying to hear all the inside stuff in the Rupert case. How about the Line-up Room at six o'clock? I'm on my way to work, so let me know tomorrow so I can arrange a sitter for Trish. Bring Peg along.*

The third caller was a man:

*Mr. Chase, this is Rex Trevellyan. My mother told me about my grandfather's cigars. I would like to have them. I'll come to your store sometime tomorrow to pick them up.*

Surprisingly, the last message was also from Hobart:

> *It's Sara again. I'm afraid I have made a fool of myself by bothering you tonight. I've thought about what I said and I've realized I was making something out of nothing. Please ignore my previous call.*

Switching off the machine, Nick grunted. Being told to ignore the first call, he thought, was like telling someone not to think about elephants. Seeking Hobart's telephone number from the service that used to be called "Information" but had taken on the exalted title "Directory Assistance," he heard a recording: "The number you requested is not available."

Feeling frustrated he was no longer endowed with the power he had enjoyed as a homicide detective to compel a phone company to give out an unlisted number, he walked into his bedroom to the muted sounds of bursts of Woolley's typing, undressed, got into bed, and ruefully replayed in his head the argument over dinner with Peg.

The ringing of his phone woke him at half past six.

# Twenty-three

ON A MAP of Cambridge the contour of Kingsley Park suggests the profile of a hound's head. Jutting into Fresh Pond, the land is encompassed on three sides by water, with the municipal golf course bordering the west edge of the pond and the town of Belmont lying beyond. Railway tracks and the north-south running Fresh Pond Parkway effectively separating the park from the city and an almost circular roadway made it idyllic for joggers, lovers, and, for the seventh time in Jack Lerch's police career, a safe place to kill someone.

In this instance the deed had been accomplished at the edge of the water on the south side of the dog's head, under cover of pea-soup fog that still hung shroudlike over park and pond and looked even more dense in the glare of floodlights. Emerging from it, Nick ducked under yellow barrier tape as Lerch said, "Sorry to roust you from bed, but I thought you should be here. You can at least confirm the identification we've made from the things we found in her purse."

A policeman in a black slicker as shiny as a beetle's back rested on one knee in the wet grass. He lifted a corner of a black plastic sheet and revealed the serene face of Sara Hobart.

"She's been dead at least seven hours," said Lerch, raising the collar of his trench coat against the cold mist. "She was manually strangled. We found nothing to indicate sexual motive. And there's nothing to suggest this was a mugging. There's money in her purse, along with credit cards. And as you can see, she's got a ring on each hand and a gold necklace. Since this wasn't a sex crime or a robbery, would you have any thoughts as to why she was murdered?''

With a shudder that was more a response to cold and damp for which he had not dressed properly than from looking death in the face, Nick said, ''The only thought I have is that she knew something about the murder of her boss. Or thought she did when she called me last night.''

Lerch signaled the kneeling policeman to re-cover the face. ''She called you?''

''Actually she left a message on my answering machine. She said she wanted to talk about something relating to the Rupert murder. But she got cold feet, phoned back, and said I should forget about her first call. I tried reaching her, but her number was unlisted.''

''What time was that?''

''That I tried reaching her? Around nine o'clock.''

''The address on her driver's license is Antrim Street, near Inman Square, so she obviously didn't come all this way because she decided to get some exercise by going out for a walk.''

Nick blew on his hands to warm them, then jammed them into the pockets of his light jacket. ''She came here to meet someone.''

''That's the way I figure it. And I think the person she met is the same man who killed her boss. Agreed?''

Nick nodded.

''If that's what happened,'' Lerch continued, ''there are two reasons for her being killed. She was either involved in Rupert's murder in some way, or she was hoping to score a payoff because she knew who did it. How well did you know her?''

''She came to my store occasionally when Rupert sent her to pick up his cigars. The last time I saw her was at the memorial in Appleton Chapel. She appeared to be in pretty bad shape. It seemed to me that she was taking Rupert's death harder than any of Rupert's family. I can't see her being directly involved in his murder. What she said on the answering machine was that she wanted to talk to me about the murder. I took her to mean that she knew something she thought had a bearing on the killing.''

Lerch grunted. ''She waited one hell of a long time to get around to mentioning it. If she'd done the right thing and told us what she knew, or thought she knew, the day Evert interviewed her, she might be alive today.''

''People don't always know the right thing, and if they do, they're often too confused, or downright scared, to speak up. Maybe something happened since Sergeant Evert talked to her that set her thinking back to that day.''

''At which point she could have started thinking of blackmail.''

''If that's what was going on, why would she call me?''

''Maybe she figured if she was going to meet with someone she ought to have protection. She thought about you being a friend of her boss, called you, then changed her mind.''

''I suppose that scenario is possible,'' Nick said as two men in coroner's office green jumpsuits appeared from the fog with a stretcher, ''but I have trouble with blackmail as a motive even in Woolley's detective novels.''

A beetle-backed policeman appeared. ''Excuse me, Lieutenant, but a couple of TV news vans just pulled up.''

Lerch sighed. ''Keep 'em at a distance till I'm outta here. And nobody's to tell them anything, including the ID. All they need to know is that we think it was a mugging.''

The officer gave a salute. ''Yes, sir.''

As he vanished in the fog, Lerch turned to Nick. ''The last thing I want right now is dealing with a bunch of newsies. I'm going to get away from them by going over to Hobart's place. Care to come along?''

With a shiver Nick said, ''How could I go back to bed now?''

Hesitating a moment before stepping from Lerch's car, Nick studied the brick front of a five-story building with graceful bay windows that once had been a single-family house. For some reason it had been split into apartments, perhaps during World War II to accommodate the sudden tide of men who had been exempted from military duty because the government had deemed their brains more useful than their bodies in a worldwide fight against tyrannies. Or maybe the conversion was made after the war when the GI Bill had opened floodgates that swamped Cambridge's colleges and universities with former combatants eager to grab a ticket to sure success in America's postwar capitalist boom—a college education.

Following Lerch up the front steps, he entered a foyer and had to sidestep to let out a young woman in a hurry. Glancing at a bank of mailboxes, he counted five, each with the name of the occupant embossed in a strip of plastic tape beneath the number of the apartment.

Under 5, Hobart's name was preceded by the sexless letter S, which, he assumed, would be how she would have listed her name in a phone book, had she not taken the even wiser step of having an unlisted number. Going up a narrow stairway, he mused on a time, long past, when a woman did not have to worry that phone books and names on letter boxes might present an opportunity to sexual predators.

This nostalgia for a better time and increasingly labored breathing as he followed Lerch upward reminded him that just as the nature of life in America had changed, Nick Chase was not the athletic detective on an old cover of *Cigar Smoker*. Slowing his pace on the climb toward the fifth floor, he puffed. "I guess Sara was in better shape than I am. These steps are killing me."

Despite a body protesting having to take the next step up, he found all the instincts of a cop were still there: the careful looks, assessing all that lay before him—wear and tear of years of feet on the navy-blue carpeting, a burned-out light bulb in a fixture on the second-floor landing, badly flaking paint on the banister between two and three, an umbrella propped against the door on the fourth. Ears tuned to every sound heard a radio set to an all-news station behind the door of the apartment on two, and a crying baby competing with a TV program on three. And the smells:

bacon cooking on the second floor, freshly brewed coffee and evidence that toast had been burned in apartment three, fresh paint on the door of apartment four, and the aroma of a cheap cigar in the hand of Sergeant Evert as he stood next to the open door of Sara Hobart's apartment on five.

Stepping toward Lerch, he said, "The building superintendent let me in." He nodded at Nick. "I had a quick look around from the doorway. Nothing inside appears to be in any way out of the ordinary."

Following Lerch, Nick stepped through the doorway and into a narrow corridor extending to the left with three closed doors he assumed were the bedroom, bath, and possibly a closet. To the right a wide doorless archway revealed a small living room.

Looking down, he found an umbrella stand. "One umbrella," he said. "I'd say she went out last night before it started raining around eight o'clock."

Evert said, "Maybe she had two umbrellas."

"Possibly, but there was no umbrella where she was found."

"She could have left it in her car."

"Also possible, but why would she take it with her and then leave it at a time when the rain was pretty heavy? I think it's more likely it wasn't raining when she left, before eight. That fits with the timing of the messages on my answering machine."

Evert blurted, "She called you last night?"

Nick nodded. "Twice, a few minutes apart, before eight. I went out at seven and played back the messages about nine. One of the calls was from my daughter. She said she was going to work. Her shift starts at eight. Since Hobart's first call was ahead of Jean's, she had to have called me before she went out and before the rain started—somewhere between seven and eight."

"What about the second call?"

"I have no way of being certain when it was made, but I think it had to be soon after the first. Jean called a little before eight. The umbrella suggests Hobart left here around the same time."

"She could have made the second call after she went out."

"That is certainly a possibility," Nick said, walking down the hallway, "but I think she made both calls from here." Opening the first two doors, he found a bathroom and closet. The third opened into a small bedroom. Entering it, he said, "I assume you guys have noticed there are no ashtrays in this apartment."

Looking round the room, Evert said, "I haven't noticed anything I didn't expect to see."

"It's been my experience," Nick said, turning to a bureau, "that the things you're not intended to find are usually tucked away somewhere." He opened the top drawer of a bureau. "When my son Kevin discovered the joys of the *Playboy* centerfold he kept his collection in the bottom of a footlocker where he stored his sports equipment. Suspicion he was hiding something was raised by the appearance of a padlock on the locker. His undoing came when he lost the key."

As Evert opened a closet door, Lerch sat on the bed next to a night table with a lamp and telephone. "What was the outcome of this small domestic crisis?"

"The term used to be a 'father-and-son chat about the birds and the bees,' " Nick replied, closing the bureau drawer, opening the one below, and finding blouses. "I was amazed that he knew so much more about sex than I knew when I was his age."

"That's because of television and movies," said Lerch as he turned on the lamp. Opening the table drawer, he found what he expected—a notepad, pencil, a thin black fake-leather address book, comb and brush, an oval-shaped mirror with a long handle, and two paperback novels with covers showing beautiful women in very low-cut dresses being embraced by beefy bare-chested men. "These days TV shows and movies are full of actors saying the F-word just because writers know they can get away with it, not to mention all the nudity and the sex scenes."

"True, true," Nick said, moving down to the third drawer and finding more blouses. "Gone are the days when a man and woman in a movie got down to doing it and the

camera turned away to show a window with curtains sway-
ing gently on a breeze, or waves lapping on a beach.'' He
closed the drawer. ''And when someone got shot in those
old movies nobody saw what a bullet does when it slams
into human flesh, either.''

Evert closed the closet door and announced, ''From the
look of her wardrobe the lady was not exactly a clothes
horse.''

Lerch replaced everything he had taken from the table
except the address book. Opening it, he muttered, ''Now
we shall see who Sara Hobart's friends were.''

''Address books can be helpful,'' said Nick, ''but I've
always thought stubs in a checkbook provide a clearer in-
sight into what was really going on in someone's life. Do
you know, Jack, if hers was among the things found with
the body?''

''No, I don't recall seeing a checkbook,'' said Lerch.
''Just her wallet.''

Evert said, ''Maybe she kept it in Rupert's office.''

''If that was the situation,'' Nick said, ''I think she
would have needed to retrieve it by now. Jack, do you
know if she has been in Rupert's store since the murder?''

Lerch shook his head. ''She couldn't have been. That
place is still under seal as a crime scene. She'd have to get
permission from me, and then I'd have had to assign someone to escort her.''

''Then the checkbook's got to be here. Okay if I have a
look around the living room, Jack?''

Lerch smiled. ''To look around is why I brought you
here.''

# Twenty-four

THE ADJECTIVE THAT popped into Nick's head as he looked into Sara Hobart's living room from the archway was "charming." White lace curtains adorning the bay windows and framing a rolltop desk provided privacy while at the same time admitting light, although on this morning of gloomy grayness the illumination was meager. Were Sara Hobart seated in the big overstuffed chair, draped with a flowery throw that faced a small fireplace, she would need to turn on a lamp to read one of four books stacked on the sturdy, square endtable that supported them and a lamp. At an angle that would also afford natural light from the windows, the chair was turned slightly toward a small fireplace in the center of a wall consisting of floor-to-ceiling shelves crammed with titles not found in Stanley Rupert's library.

To Nick's right as he stepped into the room was a couch covered with a larger throw of the same design as the chair's. Directly facing the wall of books and fireplace, it stood against a wall that seemed as cluttered with framed photographs as the walls of Rupert's bedroom. Among them he found several of Sara and Rupert that had been taken over a period of years in London, Venice, Rome, Paris, and other places where a man in the antiques business might be expected to go.

Shattering the silence of the room and causing Nick to

jerk with surprise, Lerch said, "Sara used to be a good-looking young woman, wouldn't you say?"

"Indeed she was."

"She seems to have traveled quite a lot with her boss."

"She *was* his assistant, Jack."

"Yes, but I wonder if all those trips were on a strictly business basis. He was a good-looking guy years ago, divorced, the kind of man a girl her age when some of these pictures were taken might see as dashing, maybe even a bit of a swashbuckler."

Nick barked a laugh. "Jack, I'm astonished to discover that gruff, cynical, homicide-detective pose you effect is nothing but a charade to cover up the fact that you are at heart a *romantic*. But suppose for the moment they were lovers at one time. I can't see what relevance that has to what's now clearly become a case of double murder. I also find it hard to believe that if one of them broke off their love affair they'd go on working together. The only things I know that are more important than affairs of the heart are money and self-preservation. Who can say what might have been going on between them? From what we've found out about Rupert and that plot he cooked up with his four army buddies, I'd say we can safely conclude that he was a pretty shady character. She must have known that about him, yet she stuck with him all these years. Maybe she was blackmailing him."

"That would explain everything," said Lerch, "including the two mysterious calls she left on your answering machine."

Nick sat on the couch. "I admit I haven't been playing the game of detective game for quite a few years, but that theory is even more complicated than one of Roger Woolley's frequently involved and tortured plots."

"Sara knew about his nefarious side and when he rejected her affections she decided to put the screws to him. Everything was going along swimmingly. Then Rupert is murdered, probably by someone he was scamming. Sara either knew or suspected who did it. Faced with the cutoff of her livelihood, she tried to feather her retirement nest by resorting to blackmail. What she got for her effort was a throttling in Kingsley Park.''

Nick took cigars from his case. "Why the phone calls to me?"

Lerch declined a cigar, stood, and began pacing the room. "I see a couple of reasons. First, as I said before, she was hoping to get you to accompany her when she went to meet with the guy she wanted to blackmail. She got your answering machine instead of you and had to say something that would spark your interest. Then she thought it over, changed her mind—or got cold feet—and left the second message telling you to forget the first.''

Nick lit his cigar, thought a moment, blew a column of smoke, pocketed the burned match, and said, "When she made the first call and got the machine, why not hang up?"

Lerch winced and rubbed his chin. "Why not hang up? That's a very good question, Nick." Dropping into the large armchair, he repeated, "Why . . . not . . . hang up? An *excellent* question.''

Nick held his cigar at arm's length and admired its imposing length and clean lines. "May I venture an answer?"

Lerch leaned forward in the chair. "Please do."

"This is nothing but guesswork, of course. But suppose the purpose of the first call was exactly what she said: She wanted to tell me what happened because she was afraid her game of blackmail was not paying off. Then *she* got a phone call inviting her to a meeting in the park. Hence the second call to me. All *guesswork*.''

Leaving the couch, he carried the cigar across the room and with a gentle tap knocked the long ash into the firepace.

"Guesswork it may be," said Lerch, settling back in the big chair, "but it has the ring of plausibility."

"If I am correct about her reason for the first call," Nick said, leaning on the fireplace mantel, "that she expected her reluctant victim to quickly find out I was looking into Rupert's murder, there's something significant we can deduce from that. Do you see what I'm getting at?''

Lerch tilted his head against the back of the big chair and closed his eyes. "If Sara counted on the killer finding out Nick Chase was looking into the murder . . ." With eyes popping wide and head jerking upright, he exclaimed, "The killer would have to be in a position to verify you were working the case."

"Right."

Lerch came out of the chair. "Are you aware of anybody who might have been sniffing around your store? Pumping Sam Gargan or Woolley for information? Maybe even following you?"

With a puff of the Upmann, Nick answered, "Except for you and Sergeant Evert, Woolley, Jonathan Little, Sam, my kids, and Peg Baron, the only person to show any interest in my connection with the case is the most brilliant interpreter of Tchaikovsky's first piano concerto since Van Cliburn wowed Russian music lovers in Moscow in 1958. But the only people Wilhelm Wieder has been killing are concert audiences. Besides, Wieder couldn't have slit Rupert's throat because the genius was otherwise engaged at the time at Symphony Hall."

Evert appeared in the archway to declare, "I've gone through every drawer, closet, and cabinet on the premises, including the refrigerator and toilet tank. How's the search going in here?"

Exchanging sheepish smiles with Lerch, Nick answered, "I'm afraid we have not been quite so diligent. In fact, I almost forgot why I came into this room."

"The object, I recall," said Lerch, "was a checkbook."

Evert gazed across the room. "Have you tried the desk?"

A moment later as Nick sat at the desk with Lerch and Evert peering over his shoulder, Evert asked, "What do you hope to find in Hobart's checkbook?"

"When you were a teenager, Sergeant," Nick said, opening the top right-hand drawer, "and I was a greenhorn cop on my first day working bunco, years before swindling got the name 'white-collar crime,' my boss pointed to a huge sign he had on the wall of the squad room. It said: FOLLOW THE MONEY. That is also a handy rule to observe when looking for a motive to murder."

"That's especially true," said Lerch, "if the investigation turns up even a hint of extortion."

Evert looked at Lerch incredulously. "You think Hobart was extorting someone? When and where did you get that amazing idea?"

Nick puffed his cigar. "A couple of minutes ago when we were sitting on the couch."

"There's a possibility," Lerch said as Nick rummaged through the drawer, "that Hobart had the goods on her darling boss and was squeezing him."

"If that's what was going on," Nick said, closing the drawer and opening the one below, "the evidence of it should be in her checkbook."

"Rupert could have paid her off in cash," said Evert. "The fifteen grand we found in his desk shows he was acustomed to doing business that way. The dough could have been for her."

"That is possible," Nick said. "But since she was already on his payroll as his assistant, I think that if she was extorting money it's more likely he'd cover it in her salary check."

"No matter how Rupert paid her," Lerch said, "the evidence should be reflected in both their financial records."

"It's a simple job for a forensic accountant to tabulate her expenses," Nick said, "and compare them with credits and debits in her bank records, as well as Rupert's accounts. Money doesn't come and go without leaving a set of footprints."

"We also think that after Rupert was suddenly taken out of the picture," Lerch said, "she grabbed the opportunity and tried to blackmail the killer."

"Judging from this apartment," Evert said, looking around the small, sparely furnished room, "Sara was not exactly living high on the hog."

"People do have more than one address," Nick said, turning to the top drawer on the left of the desk. "Who'd have thought Jerome Lazarus owned a waterfront cottage on the Cape?"

Lerch said, "We are dealing with a woman. We may find that Sara Hobart decided to ensure a comfortable old age by collecting diamonds and blue-chip stocks."

Nick exclaimed, "Ah ha," and plunging a hand in the

drawer, he pulled out the checkbook. ''Now it's up to your financial analysts figure out how Sara Hobart's bank account jibes with the books and ledgers Rupert maintained for his business.''

Lerch pocketed the checkbook. ''I'm betting they will.'' Leaving the desk, Nick said, ''Now, if you'll excuse me, I am going home to have breakfast. And then I've got a store to open.''

# Twenty-five

CLOSING THE WHITE door, Nick paused a moment in semi-darkness and silence to absorb and appreciate the aromas of tobaccos: Virginia, also called Bright, discovered by English settlers in the land of Pocahontas, with subtle sweetness and delicate fruitiness; Maryland, with a rich brown coloring and bland flavor that increased burning properties of other tobaccos; Burley, mainly a product of Tennessee, Kentucky, and Ohio—extremely light-tasting and readily mixed; almost-black Latakia from Syria providing rich and heavy flavor; Perique, so strong that only a truly courageous smoker would try it by itself; Turkish, a category including all the tobaccos of the Far East; aromatics in which nontobacco substances were added to flavor and sweeten; and the tobaccos of cigars, smoked by natives of the so-called New World long before the Europeans arrived, and now grown almost everywhere, from the Caribbean islands to Sumatra and the Connecticut River Valley.

In fifteen years he had learned not only about tobaccos, but that a cigar store's day unfolded in stages.

It started with the dispelling of the night's darkness when he turned on the lights. These consisted of unintrusive recessed ceiling fixtures and a scattering of floor and table lamps that offered pools of illumination which created a cozy tranquillity for smokers who paused a moment in the rush from homes to jobs for one cigar or a day's worth.

Very much as he had been when he was a cop on the way to a day shift, they were usually wordless. Except for "Good morning," "Hello," or the name of their brand, it was in and out.

From then to lunch hour the rhythm of the store was slower as the fewer customers seemed eager for and even solicitous of unrushed conversation beyond that needed to survey the choices of cigars available, to select, and perhaps to buy.

Between noon and roughly two o'clock the mood became clubby as it resonated with baritone voices expressing no sense of hurry or urgency, nor for some any intention of making a purchase. At this time the store seemed to be brimming with all the camaraderie and bonhommie promised by the golden letters on the green sign on the storefront—very much like being in a New York City cop bar after a shift when he was a bachelor.

Midafternoon, he had learned, was the time for students and professors mingling with the occasional tourist exploring Harvard Yard and Square and historic sites that pocket maps of Cambridge pinpointed along Brattle Street.

From approximately four o'clock to six or seven as the tide flowed from jobs to homes, customers were relaxed and more likely to linger over decisions. Occasionally a novice smoker, or even a veteran wishing to widen the experience, asked for advice. Of all the quesions posed in his decade and a half behind the old cash register, the most common was which cigar would be best suited to accompany cocktails before dinner or a brandy after.

When a woman came in she was usually acting for a man in her life—husband, lover, brother, dad, grandfather, uncle, perhaps an employer, as Sara Hobart had done so often.

Or, he thought as he glanced at the Rudyard Kipling poem on the subject of women and cigars hanging on the wall, to placate a temperamental piano player.

As he went behind the cash register to light an Upmann in anticipation of the unfolding of the first of the day's stages, the phone rang.

"Hello," he answered brightly. "The Happy Smoking Ground."

The brusqueness of the caller left no doubt that it was not his son on the line, but Kevin Chase the crime reporter.

"A reliable source has told me that a dead woman found in Kingsley Park this morning worked for a certain murdered antiques dealer," Kevin said. "My source also said you were there. True?"

"If your source is so *reliable*," Nick replied, cradling the receiver between neck and shoulder and using both hands to trim the cigar, "why are you bothering me?"

Kevin sighed. "May I construe your answer as a yes?"

"Who am I to tell you what you can construe? You're thirty-five years old and—"

"Thirty-seven."

"You are old enough to construe to your heart's content, but the only thing I am confirming is that The Happy Smoking Ground is now open for what I hope will be a very good day for business. How are you, Noreen, and my grandchildren?"

"I'm sure we'd all feel a lot better if you'd stop showing up at the scene every time there's another murder in town."

"The woman in the park was murdered?"

"Don't play the coy cop with me, Dad. You know damn well it was murder. And we both know who the victim is. *Was*."

"If you know all this why are you questioning me?"

"I'm not *questioning* you."

"Well, you sure fooled me."

"Will you answer me off the record?"

"That depends on what you ask."

"Were you in the park and then at the woman's home?"

"Off the record and old man to son: Your source is correct on the matter of me being in both places."

"Off the record, father to son: What about the identity of the woman? It was Rupert's assistant, Sara Hobart, correct?"

"Again, you may put your trust in your source."

"Thank you very much."

"Now may I put an off-the-record question to you?"

"Fire away."

"Who's this reliable source of yours?"

"Dad, you know I can't reveal that. Journalistic ethics—"

"There's a debatable term!"

"I cannot disclose a source, even to you, Dad."

"I'm merely seeking confirmation of what I already know."

"You think you know my source?"

"I don't *think* I know. I *know*. Would you like me tell you?"

After a slight pause, Kevin said, "I'm listening."

"Your source is a sergeant with Lerch's homicide squad by the name of Gary Evert."

Kevin laughed nervously. "You're guessing."

"Oh no, my boy. You asked if it was true that I was in the park *and* in the dead woman's home. There were three people in the apartment. Two were policemen. One was Jack Lerch, who has never been a reporter's source in his life. The other was Sergeant Gary Evert. I know the third man was not your source, so ergo and ipso facto, Evert is your snitch. I rest my case. Now, a word of fatherly advice: When talking to a cop, even one who has been out of the harness for a good many years, be careful what you say."

"May I ask you another question as a son?"

"I hope this isn't going to prove as embarrassing for me as our talk about the birds and bees."

"I understand how you happened onto the scene of the first murder. But it's obvious you were not just passing by Kingsley Park. Lerch summoned you there."

"That's a statement," Nick said as stage one's first customer came in. An employee of a small bookstore in nearby Eliot Square who favored a Romeo y Julieta Brevas, he smiled, nodded in greeting, and went straight to where they were kept. With a smile in return, Nick asked Kevin, "What is your question?"

"Are you working with Lerch on these murders?"

"Am I on the Cambridge Police Department payroll? No," Nick said as the customer brought six cigars to the counter. "Have I been of use to Lerch as a source of information? That remains to be seen. I certainly hope so.

May we end this call, please? I've got a customer waiting.''

"Sure, Dad. Take care.''

"This conversation was off the record, right?''

Kevin chuckled. "What conversation?''

With the Romeo y Julieta man tucking the Brevas into a small silver pocket case and going out the door, Nick reviewed what he had told Kevin, satisfied himself he had not provided more information than he got, and realized with relief that Evert evidently had made no mention of Sara Hobart's two messages.

Remembering the calls had bracketed one by his daughter, he picked up the phone, dialed Jean's number, found himself answered by her recording machine, and told it he would be delighted to have dinner with Jean and Mike Tinney Saturday night.

A moment after he put down the phone the door opened and a cluster of customers set stage one of the day in full but almost silent animation. They and subsequent smokers during the next hour and a half selected cigars singly, by the handful, and in two instances in boxes of twenty-five. They came to the counter with cash or credit cards and took away Caballeros Rothchilds, Casa Blanca Panatelas, and Don Leo Cetros made in the Dominican Republic, Hinds Brothers Royal Coronas from Honduras, a variety of Macanudos, Mexico's famous and popular Te-Amo, and a few nonpremium, machine-made, packaged Garcia y Vega, King Edward, and Antonio y Cleopatra.

With stage one over by nine o'clock, he looked through the bay window and saw Roger Woolley striding toward the white door. Realizing with horror that he had not thought to inform the old man of Sara's murder, he concluded with relief from Woolley's smile when the old man came in that he had not yet learned of it.

Moving as gracefully as a tall-masted sailing ship, he was dressed in a blue blazer, gray slacks, and white shirt open to reveal an emerald-green neckerchief. Smoking his new pipe and jauntily swinging an ebony walking stick with a silver swan's head, he was across the store to the counter in three strides. "I am in desperate need of pipe tobacco.''
Seeing Nick's drawn expression, he jerked the pipe from

his mouth. "You look absolutely dreadful. Something terrible has happened!"

Nick nodded slowly. "I'm afraid so."

Woolley tapped the floor with his stick. "It's Sara Hobart, isn't it? She's dead."

Nick's expression went from glum to surprised. "Yes, she is. How and when did you hear about it?"

"I did not know until now. But I feared after she called me that she would be the next one to meet such a fate."

Nick's surprise became astonishment. "When did she call you?"

Woolley carefully placed both pipe and stick on the glass countertop. "Last evening, around a quarter to eight. The dear thing was very excited. She asked for your phone number."

"You should have informed Lerch."

"You know how I feel about that man."

"How you feel about him is irrelevant. He's the detective on the case."

Woolley scooped up pipe and stick and headed for the door. "I gather Sara did not speak to you."

"She tried, but she got my answering machine. Unfortunately, she chose not to leave a number."

"Horrible devices. I would never have one," said Woolley, standing at the door with his walking stick slack in his grip. "I suppose I'd better telephone Millie Trevellyan about this before she learns of it in some other way. This news is going to be as much a horrible shock for her as it has been for me."

"Why should Millicent Trevellyan be upset?"

"They'd always been close. I had a feeling that Sara saw in Millicent the daughter she might have had if it had been herself rather than Rebecca whom Stanley married."

"Rex also left me a message last night," Nick said. "He'll be dropping by today to pick up the cigars Rupert left in his locker in the humidor room. Four boxes of Montecristo Churchills."

Woolley sighed deeply. "All this death is so sad, isn't it? First it was the murder of Stanley, then Lazarus's suicide, and now the saddest of them all—dear Sara. The death of anyone is the stuff of tragedy, but as Edgar Allan Poe observed, the death of a beautiful woman is the most poetical topic in the world.''

For stage three of The Happy Smoking Ground's day, Nick was joined by Sam Gargan in dealing with customers spending lunchtime in relaxed and leisurely browsing of stock and smoking while they debated the virtues of various brands. Also discussed heatedly were the state of the hockey season and the fading of the Bruins' chances of reaching the Stanley Cup playoffs. Others spoke sadly of dim prospects for the Red Sox, already far down in divisional rankings in a baseball season that was barely under way. Neither a customer nor Sam, Nick was pleased to observe, had anything to say to him about a woman murdered in Kingsley Park.

An hour after the noontime rush ended and Sam Gargan left for afternoon classes, the till of the old cash register already contained enough cash and credit card receipts to make the day profitable. Seated on a tall stool behind the counter, smoking his third Upmann, and leafing through the catalog of a wholesale dealer in cigar accoutrements, Nick heard the door open. Looking up, he was surprised to find Wilhelm Wieder.

Wearing faded blue jeans, sneakers, a Red Sox baseball cap, and a gray sweatshirt imprinted with HARVARD ATHLETIC DEPT, he said, ''Hello, Nick. I was in the neighborhood to see my brother and thought I'd drop in to say hello.''

''That's very kind of you. What's your brother studying?''

''I can tell you what he's supposed to be studying. At times I have the distinct impression he's majoring in a combined course of ice hockey, sex, and music, if you can call rock and roll music.''

''Your brother doesn't appreciate classical music?''

''Friedrich appreciates its benefits in the form of my checks for tuition, board, books, and meals in expensive restaurants, not to forget covering his credit card purchases at the Harvard Co-op and in shopping malls all over New

England. The only expensive taste he has yet to indulge is cigars.''

"You prefer Montecristo Churchills, I recall."

"That's my other purpose in being here. If you're out of the Churchills, Lonsdales or Coronas will do."

"A cigar dealer who runs out of Montecristos," Nick said, entering the humidor room, "will soon be out of business."

Following him, Wieder said, "I'll take four boxes of twenty-five, if I may. I'm going to New Hampshire, Vermont, and Maine for a week of college recitals and don't want to chance running out."

"I believe there are cigar stores in those states, too."

"But not as fine as your establishment, I'm sure. The Happy Smoking Ground! What a clever and charming name."

Nick took four boxes from a shelf. "Thank you. My daughter suggested it. I was going to call the place Nick's Tobacco Shop. Not very imaginative, but succinct."

"My compliments to your daughter."

Carrying the cigars to the counter, Nick said, "She enjoyed your concert at Symphony Hall."

"I'm so sorry you were not able to attend."

Nick rang up the sale. "Recalling what happened that Monday night, so am I."

Wieder produced a gold credit card. "I hope one day before I return to England at the end of the month that you'll have solved the murder and will come to lunch in my suite at the Copley Plaza Hotel to tell me all about it."

As his credit card was being processed, Nick said, "It's the police who will solve the case. It is not my investigation."

"Are the police making any progress?"

Nick returned the card. "I can't say."

Wieder signed the purchase slip. "You can't say? Or you do not wish to say?"

Nick smiled. "How could I possibly comment on something I know nothing about?"

Wieder let out a laugh. "Some music critics I know do so all the time. But your friend Peg assures me those in

Vermont, New Hampshire, and Maine are not in that category. What a delight she is.''

''Peg's a sweetie, all right.''

''I don't know how I could manage to get through this tour without her advice and counsel. She has not only been kind enough to make the arrangements for next week's trip, she is traveling with me to ensure that, as she put it, I don't end up some place in Canada.''

''That's typical of her. She goes all out for the thing she loves most—music.''

''She certainly loves that,'' Wieder said while Nick put the boxes into a paper tote bearing the name of the store arranged in a semicircle above a drawing of the wooden Indian outside the door. ''However, as I've come to know her in the past two weeks or so, I've learned that music is not foremost in her heart. I hope I'm not out of line in saying that she has reserved that distinction for a certain cigar store proprietor.''

''You're right. You are out of line. Damn rude, actually.''

Wieder took the bag and strode toward the door. ''That is a quality, I must admit, that is inherent to the Teutonic nature.'' Pausing with a hand on the latch, he added,'' Therefore, I feel emboldened to say that I have been astonished by the disgraceful manner with which you seem to treat a woman who is a lady in every way. There's a word in German for such a man: *schufte*.''

Nick glowered. ''When I went to school in the 1940s, German was no longer in the curriculum. I'm sure you understand why.''

''It means cad. But here's an adjective you should find easy to understand,'' Wieder said, going out. ''*Dumm*.''

Minutes before the seven o'clock closing time, still bridling with anger at Wieder's presumptiveness, Nick lit his last cigar of the business day as Rex Trevellyan barged through the door.

''Good, you're still here,'' he exclaimed. ''I was afraid you wouldn't be open.'' Wearing a tuxedo, he bore a resemblance to his grandfather that Nick had not fully appre-

ciated at the memorial service. "Am I too late to pick up
the cigars?"

"Not at all, but are you sure you want to lug around four
boxes of cigars when you're dressed to the nines? What's
the big occasion?"

"I'm hosting a bachelor party at the Hotel Commander
for my cousin Harry."

"Ah yes. Your grandfather's nephew."

"Do you know him?"

"Professor Woolley pointed him out to me at the memorial for your grandfather."

"It was very good of you to attend."

"Stan was a friend and valued customer. It will take just
a moment to get the cigars," Nick said, balancing the Upmann on the edge of the counter. "They're in his private
locker in the humidor room."

Rex looked at him with an alarmed expression. "I didn't
know he had a locker. I'm sorry, I don't have the key and
I have not a clue where it might be."

"No matter," Nick said, going into the humidor. "I've
got a master key to the lockers."

Rex sighed. "Oh good."

"You'd be amazed how many men forget to bring theirs.
Others always seem to misplace or lose them."

"I've never given any thought to keeping my supply
anyplace but in my humidor at home," Rex said as he
followed Nick to the door of the room. "What happens if
people run out and your store is closed?"

"If they live nearby, which most of my customers do,"
Nick said, taking a ring of keys from his jacket pocket,
"they phone me and we arrange to meet here."

"That's very nice of you."

"It's no big deal. I live upstairs."

"Be that as it may, it's got to be an imposition."

"In a time of crisis, a proper tobacconist expects to be
imposed on," Nick said, unlocking Rupert's locker.
"There's a story about Alfred Dunhill telephoning Prime
Minister Churchill after a Nazi bombing raid on London to
tell him not to worry, the humidor room was undamaged,
and Mr. Churchill's cigars were safe. As you know, thanks

to Churchill's inspiring leadership and words during the war, so was England.''

''I regret to say that when I was in school I was not a very good student of history.''

Nick winced. ''The Second World War may be history to you, young man, but I remember it very well.''

''You were a soldier?''

''It was men of your grandfather's generation who fought it. I went from age seven at the time of Pearl Harbor to twelve at war's end,'' Nick said, reaching into Rupert's locker. ''But even for a kid, the war was very real. I followed it on the radio and in the newsreels at the movies. It's a pity Stan didn't live to attend his nephew's wedding.''

''If grandfather were still alive, Harry's wedding would be the last place I would expect to see him.''

Sliding the stacked cigar boxes from the locker, Nick found a large, white, slightly bulging envelope imprinted with Rupert's business address and on the front in black fountain pen ink and bold letters:

### FOR NICK CHASE
### TO BE OPENED ONLY IN THE EVENT
### THAT I WAS MURDERED

Startled and hoping Rex had not seen the envelope, Nick left it in place, held the cigar boxes in his right hand, and shut the locker door. Carrying them to Rex, he said with forced cheerfulness, ''Here you go, young man. A hundred Montecristo Churchills.''

Taking them, Rex asked, ''How much do I owe you?''

''They're all bought and paid for. I hope when you smoke them you will do so with fond memories of your grandfather.''

''That's a sweet sentiment, Mr. Chase,'' Rex said as Nick left the humidor room, ''but I'm sure Woolley has informed you that my grandfather and I were not very close. The fact is, I hadn't seen him for well over a year, and then for only a very brief moment, which was not a pleasant one. None of our meetings were.''

''I'm sorry you two didn't get along.''

"As for these cigars, they're not my brand," Rex said on his way out of the store. "I prefer Partagas. These are for the guests at Harry's party." He stopped at the door and smiled. "Is that not a perfectly wonderful irony?"

With Rex gone Nick muttered, "Snotty little twerp," locked the front door, rushed into the humidor room, opened the locker, and pulled out the envelope. When he ripped it open a bronze key fell into his palm. Removing a single sheet of paper with handwriting in the same black ink as the enevlope, he read:

*Dear Nick,*

*That you are reading this means that I was not able to prevent my murder. Because you are a brilliant detective I am sure you have figured out that my talk about the Columbus diary was my trick to get you to come to my store. My intent was to have you present in case there was trouble and I had to defuse a potentially dangerous situation by buying my way out of it.*

*In view of the fact that you are reading this letter, my plan obviously went awry, as such schemes do, not only when at first we practice to deceive, but when we make deception the custom of a lifetime.*

*Enclosed with this note you will find the key to an antique strongbox. It is located in the window at the front of my store and has a red "Sold" tag. All you need to understand what led to my murder is explained in a letter in the strongbox. It contains material that may be useful in your investigation of my murder, and as evidence.*

*I am counting on you to do the right thing for the foolish man who speaks to you from the merciful oblivion of death.*

*Yours truly,*
*Stanley Rupert*

# PART IV

## A Rare Old Cigar Box

# Twenty-six

HALF AN HOUR after finding Rupert's astonishing letter, Nick watched as Jack Lerch, followed by Gary Evert, crossed the sidewalk in front of Stanley Rupert's store with the same purposeful manner he had shown on the night of Rupert's murder.

Lerch gave Nick a quick nod of greeting.

"Evening, Jack," Nick said, handing him the envelope with the letter and strongbox key. "Sorry I interrupted your dinner."

"In all my years as a murder cop," Lerch said, pulling the letter from the envelope, "I've never had a case where before the victim met his fate, he wrote a letter that pointed out where the evidence to crack the case could be found."

As Lerch read the letter, Nick said, "Jack, no one is more flabbergasted by this than I. But everything in it certainly fits with what happened that night: the fear he felt, why he sat up Sunday night with a gun in his hand, why he arranged to have me come to the store, even the fifteen grand in cash in the desk drawer he hoped to use, as he said in the letter, to buy his way out of a dangerous situation."

"It sounds like a blackmail case to me," Lerch said, looking past Nick and into the display window. "There's the box with the red ''Sold'' tag, all right."

Looking extremely old, the rectangular metal box had a dark patina of years of encrusted grime, slightly rusted narrow strips of reinforcing metal bands, and a curved top. Closed with a padlock that seemed new, the chest appeared smaller than a tin breadbox that Nick remembered in his mother's kitchen.

As he followed the detectives into the store and Evert threw a switch to turn on the ceiling lights, glassy eyes of the stuffed and mounted deer and elk heads seemed to be scrutinizing them.

"I don't mind telling you," Evert said softly, "that I feel very damn spooky about this."

As Lerch took the strongbox from the window display, Nick said, "I don't think we have to talk in whispers, Sergeant."

After unlocking the padlock and opening the lid of the box, Lerch peered inside the chest and grunted. "What we have here, Nick," he declared as he removed the only object in the chest, "is right up your alley."

Made of cardboard and coated with paper intended to look like cedar wood, the box's lid bore an oval imprinted with red ink and within it the name of the brand and style of the fifty cigars it had once contained: Sherlock Holmes Crooks. Turning the box upside down, Nick noted the long-since smoked cigars had been handmade in a factory in Pennsylvania. A rectangle of red lettering advised the original purchaser:

The cigars herein contained were manufactured to retail at more than 4c each and not more than 6c each and are so tax paid.

Another statement appeared below:

## FACTOR No. 3                        1st DIST PA.

*Notice: The manufacturer of the cigars herein contained has complied with all the requirements of law. Every person is cautioned not to use either this box for cigars again or the stamp thereon again. Nor to remove the contents of this box without destroying said stamp under the penalties provided by law in such cases.*

"I wouldn't mind having this in my Holmes collection," said Nick as he turned back the lid and found a color portrait of the actor William Gillette, who had built a career portraying Holmes on the stage. Surrounded on two sides by gold leaves and above by SHERLOCK HOLMES in green and gold, the stern-faced figure had on a gray deerstalker cap. In the box lay a small but bulky manila clasp envelope. "Since this is your case, Jack," Nick said as he returned the box to Lerch, "I think you're the one who should see what's in the envelope."

"Yeah, right," Lerch said, taking the box. "But not here in the window. We'll do it in Rupert's office." On the way, he looked at the cluttered store and said, "I'd hate to be the guy who's going to have to clear out all this stuff."

"Since Woolley's the executor of the estate," Nick replied, "I imagine he'll take the easy way and bring in another antiques dealer. Perhaps Jonathan Little. If Woolley hires an auctioneer you may luck out, Jack, and grab a real bargain. You might even be the winning bidder on the roll-top desk in the window. You said you always wanted one."

"If I brought that thing home," Lerch said, going into the office, "my wife would either divorce or kill me. Old furniture is not to her taste. She trades in our living room suite every five years, whether it needs it or not. But if I dare suggest that we go to Filene's and get a set of slipcovers she looks at me as if I were some kind of barbarian."

Entering Rupert's office, Nick noticed that a large, square section of the bloodstained Oriental had been cut out and taken away by a criminalist. Splotches of shiny gray powder indicated the work of fingerprint lifters. Missing from the desktop was the ashtray, taken as evidence along with the two Montecristo boxes.

Sitting at Rupert's desk, Lerch opened the envelope. Fishing out the contents one item at a time, he laid on the desk a sheet of folded paper, a brass key, and a booklet with a paper cover in gray. In its center and embossed in gold and black an eagle with outstretched wings grasped in its talons a circular laurel wreath with a red swastika in the middle.

"Damn it all," Lerch grumbled, handing it to Nick, "don't tell me we're back to square one and that crazy Nazi business."

Examining the booklet, Nick smiled. "We sure are, Jack, but not to square one. Do you realize what this is?"

"Offhand, I'd say it's the identification book that belonged to the Nazi that Rupert and his buddies executed."

Nick turned to Evert. "Sergeant, give the man a cigar."

Lerch picked up the paper and unfolded it. "I would also say that this is a copy of that compact those loonies drew up."

Nick frowned. "There should be two. Rupert's and Sid Gold's. Unless Gold's *was* on him the day he drowned. If that's the case the one Rupert made a show of burning was a fake. But this paper is nowhere nearly as signficant as the photograph in this ID."

"I fail to see what a picture of a man who's been dead for half a century has to do with any of this," Lerch said, picking up the key that had fallen from the envelope. "And what the hell is this all about?"

Evert spoke up. "It looks like the kind of key I have for my bank safe deposit box. If that's what it is, it can be traced."

"Then get to it right away," Lerch said, handing it to him.

"The banks are closed, boss."

"Then check it out first thing tomorrow."

"I'll need a court order."

"*Then find a judge and get one.* I want to know what's in it. I can only hope it turns out not to be another damn souvenir of an event that, as far as I'm concerned, as bad as the Second World War was, is long-ago history. Hell, today the richest people in America wear designer clothes by Versace and shoes by Gucci made in Italy, drive around in BMWs, Mercedes, Volkswagens, and Subarus, and the rest of us watch TV and play back rented movies on VCRs that are all made in Japan! Tell me, Nick, who the hell won that war anyway?"

"Millions of GIs like my late brother-in-law Bob."

With pink embarassment overspreading his face, Lerch

said, "I'm sorry, Nick. This case is getting me so pissed off that I'm shooting off my big mouth without thinking. Now, what's so damn important about the picture of a dead Nazi officer named . . . What's it say in his ID?"

"The name in it is Weiderhoffer. Professor Woolley called him Kadiddlehopper, after the character on the Red Skelton show. As to the photo, if you can spare a little more of your evening to make a trip across the river you can judge the significance of it yourself."

Lerch rubbed his chin. "Don't I get even a hint?"

Nick pocketed the ID. "I don't want to prejudice you."

After crossing the Charles River via the Harvard Bridge and turning left into Boylston Street, they proceeded in a straight line for six blocks to swing right into the triangle of Copley Plaza. With the lofty grandeur of Trinity Church facing west and on the right the stolid stone classicism of Boston Public Library with its six broad steps, arches, great bronze doors, and interior court in the style of an Italian *palazzo*, they headed toward one of America's finest grand hotels.

"The Copley Plaza," declared Lerch, parking in front. "Did you know, Nick, that I spent my wedding night in this hotel?"

"Is there a commemorative plaque?"

"Very droll, my friend. But after what that single night of connubial bliss cost me, there ought to be."

Getting out of the car, Nick looked at the elegant facade. "I hope the man we've come to see is at home."

"I haven't a clue to what you're up to, Nick," Lerch said as they entered the hotel, "but your instincts have served well this far. If he's not in we'll wait."

## *Twenty-seven*

WHEN THE DOOR to suite 1212 opened, Wilhelm Wieder had on the sweatshirt and jeans he had worn earlier, but sneakers had been exchanged for slippers.

"Nick," he exclaimed. "What a surprise to see you so soon. I don't believe I've met these two gentlemen."

"This is Detective Jack Lerch and his partner Sergeant Gary Evert," Nick said. "We were going to dinner in the vicinity, and I was telling them of your deep interest in the progress of the investigation, so we decided to drop in on you and give you an update. I hope we haven't picked a bad time."

"Not at all," said Wieder, extending a hand to Lerch. "I am delighted to meet you, sir. And you, too, Sergeant Evert. Please, do come in."

The large room had a fireplace flanked by a red wing chair and a pair of sofas done in royal blue and gold. A large cocktail table between them was littered with musical scores. In a corner stood a gleaming black Steinway grand piano.

"Excuse the untidiness of the parlor," Wieder said as he led them to the sofas. "I have been reviewing the pieces I will be performing on my tour. May I get you something to drink?"

Nick shook his head and lied. "I've already passed my limit of drinks in one night."

Lerch followed Nick's lead. "And Sergeant Evert and I never drink while we're working."

Wieder's black eyebrows arched quizically. "You are on duty this evening?"

"Well, so to speak," Lerch said as he, Nick, and Lerch sat on the sofas. "In the homicide business detectives are always expected to be on call. If you have to respond to a crime scene it's better if you show up sober."

Wieder nodded gravely and sat in the chair. "It must be an arduous profession, but a very rewarding one when you've finally caught a killer."

"There's a certain satisfaction."

"But I imagine investigating a real-life murder is not in the least like the ones I sometimes see on television programs and in films. They always make it appear so easily done."

"You're right. If Stanley Rupert's murder happened on TV it would be solved in an hour."

"With time out for commercials," Evert added.

"We've been dealing with the Rupert case going on a couple of weeks," Lerch said, "but I am sorry to say there is still no light at the end of the tunnel."

"Since I met Nick," Wieder said, "I have followed the case in the newspapers with intense interest."

"So I've been told."

"I will be terribly disappointed if you have not solved it before I have to return to England."

Lerch made a sour face. "So will I."

"But surely you are not at a complete impasse?"

"The case has not been without surprises. Matter of fact, we ran into one this evening."

"Fascinating," Wieder said, looking questioningly at Nick. "Can you tell me what it was? Or am I to be left to dangle on tenterhooks?"

Nick's hand went into a pocket and withdrew the ID book. "They say a picture is worth a thousand words," he said, handing it to Wieder. "Have a look at this."

Wieder stared for a moment at the red swastika, opened the book with trembling hands, gazed at the photo, and with a choking voice said, "This is quite remarkable." He looked up at Nick with swimming eyes. ''I am utterly flab-bergasted.''

''So was I,'' said Nick.

''Where did you find this?''

''You do recognize the man in the picture?''

Wieder nodded slowly.

''I thought you might,'' Nick said. ''I spotted the resemblance immediately. I suspect you did, too.''

Wieder smiled. ''It is quite extraordinary.''

''If I didn't know that photo is well over fifty years old,'' Nick said, ''I'd swear it was taken of *you* yesterday.''

''Or of my brother. Actually, it's even more like him.''

''Just for the record,'' Lerch said, ''will you identify the man in that picture for us?''

''Certainly. He was my grandfather.''

''The name in that ID is Wiederhoffer.''

''As Nick knows, my parents changed the family name.''

Lerch said, ''If my grandfather had been an officer in one of Hitler's death camps I would certainly lose no time changing my name, either.''

Wieder's eyes narrowed with anger. ''My grandfather did *not* serve in any death camp. He was an officer of the *Wehrmacht*, the regular army! He was killed in the closing weeks of the Second World War in action against the Russians as the Red Army closed in on Berlin.'' He turned to Nick. ''I don't know how you came by this amazing document—''

''It was discovered among Stanley Rupert's possessions,'' said Nick. ''It was one of several war souvenirs. I'm sorry, but there is no question your grandfather was a captain in the SS. Rupert shot him to death when he was trying to escape from a camp named Ohrdruf Nord near the town of Gotha. There is no doubt. We have a document proving it. And we have an eyewitness who will verify that ID book, and the man pictured in it was the officer Rupert killed. We even have your grandfather's Luger pistol.''

Weider shifted nervously in the chair. ''This is very interesting, Nick, but what exactly are you driving at?''

''I'm driving at a possible motive for Rupert's murder.''

''What motive?''

"One of the oldest of all. Revenge."

"Revenge for what?"

"For the murder of your grandfather. That's how he died; not fighting the Red Army as you were undoubtedly led to believe, but in an act of cold-blooded murder. I have no idea how you might have come to know that Rupert was the one who shot him near that death camp. But I find it hard to accept your being in Boston the very night that Rupert was murdered was coincidence."

"First, I had never heard of this man Rupert. Secondly, you know that at the time he was killed I was at Symphony Hall!"

"What I do *not* know is what your younger brother was doing at that time."

"Are you actually accusing my brother of this murder?"

"He appears to have had a motive. As a student at Harvard he certainly had opportunity. And the means in the form of a knife at hand in the store."

Wieder burst into laughter. "Oh, my dear Nick, if you have settled on my brother as your suspect, you are terribly mistaken. He definitely was not in that antiques shop that night."

"You were at Symphony Hall. How can you say where he was and what he was doing at the time?"

"Permit me to answer by repeating that neither I nor he had ever heard of this man Rupert. Furthermore, it was my manager who well over a year ago arranged my appearance in concert with the BSO. At that time my brother had been a student at Harvard for two years and had not been back to England in more than a year. I welcomed the chance to come over to Boston not only to advance my career, but as an opportunity to visit with him. That I was here at the time of the murder was, therefore, a coincidence. But even if my brother and I had known of that man and wished to kill him out of revenge, the deed could have been done at any time during the past two years. Finally, I am not the only person who knows my brother could not have murdered Mr. Rupert. There is someone who can provide what the police call an ironclad alibi."

Lerch demanded, "Who is that person?"

Wieder smiled slyly. "Nick's friend Peg Baron."

Nick's eyes went wide. "What?"

"Ask Peg and she will tell you that during the concert she was seated right beside my brother. She had a pair of tickets, but the man she had invited to the concert had something more important to do, as you well know Nick. Although my brother had a ticket of his own, Peg insisted he sit in the seat next to hers. She will also tell you that they were backstage visiting with me in my dressing room during the intermission. I invite you to use my telephone to call her and confirm this."

"I don't believe that's necessary at the moment."

"An accusation of murder has been made. I demand you make a call to Peg right now."

As Nick reluctantly rose from the sofa, Lerch caught him by a sleeve. "I'll handle it, Nick. This *is* a police matter."

"No, Jack, I made the accusation, I'll make the call."

As unmoving and silent as the wooden Indian in front of The Happy Smoking Ground, Wieder, Evert and Lerch listened to Nick's side of the conversation: "Peg, it's Nick . . . I'm not calling at a bad time I hope . . . Yes, I know you're miffed at me, but that's not why I'm callling . . . The concert you went to the night Stan Rupert was murdered, you told me you had two tickets . . . For a reason I'll explain to you tomorrow, I need to know now what you did with the other one . . . I see . . . Thanks. Yes, I *will* call you tomorrow. Right now I have to apologize to somebody. Bye."

As Nick put down the telephone, Wieder stood and extended a hand. "Your apology is accepted."

"Thank you. I'm glad I was wrong. We'll let you get back to the work we interrupted."

"Not so fast, my friend," Wieder said. "I believe I and my brother are entitled to know the entire chain of events that has led to a moment of high drama that certainly rivals anything in my experience since I first sat through Richard Wagner's *Der Ring des Nibelungen*. The difference between then and now is that I am old enough to smoke cigars. Take all the time you need. I happen to have four fresh boxes of Montecristo Churchills."

"It's not a long story," Nick said, returning to the sofa and thinking of five Americans and a chance encounter with a man who would never know that his grandson would become a virtuoso on the piano. As Wieder offered them cigars, Nick sighed and said, "I'm sorry to say the tale has no heroes."

Half an hour later with Nick in the backseat, Lerch started the car and looked at Nick reflected in the rearview mirror. "Did you notice that look of amazement on Wieder's face when you got to the part about the buried treasure?"

"I was more interested in his expression that indicated he'd accepted the evidence his grandfather was a war criminal. I can't begin to imagine what Wieder must be thinking right now."

"My guess is he's thinking of how that treasure might have made the Weiderhoffers very, very rich."

"I don't think so," Nick said as the car moved away from the curb. "He's probably trying to come to terms with the fact that during his entire life he was made to believe he was the grandson of a hero-defender of the Fatherland against the Red Army."

Negotiating turns around the small triangular park that was the heart of Copley Square, Lerch said, "Made to believe? I say he *chose* to believe it."

"Pardon me, Jack," Nick said, leaning forward, "but I can't see how you can make such an outrageous assumption."

"That young man is no fool, Nick. For anyone that smart the change of the family name had to be a tipoff something was amiss in the ancestral history."

"Wieder simply fit better on a marquee than Wiederhoffer."

"Your rationalization fails on two points," Lerch said as Nick settled back. "First, the name was changed long before the kid ever became a star in the world of classical music. Second, people who put names on marquees never seem to have a problem in fitting Shostakovich and a slew of others with long names onto concert hall marquees and posters.''

As the car left Copley Square, Nick sat silent. But as Lerch negotiated a curve to put them onto Harvard Bridge, he declared, ''Whether Wieder knew the truth about his grandfather before tonight does not alter the fact that he and his brother had nothing to do with Rupert's murder.'' He paused and gazed through at the lights of Boston and Cambridge reflected on the broad black expanse of the Charles River basin. ''Frankly, I should have known the Wieders were not behind the Rupert murder for no other reason than they had no motive for the second one,'' he continued. ''The next time that I'm charging around like a bull in a china shop, whisper in my ear the name of Sara Hobart. Rupert's murder was coolly planned. Hers was necessary to ensure the killer got away with the first, which so far he is succeeding in doing while the case grows colder and time marches relentlessly on.''

''You know there is no statute of limitations on murder.''

''True, but there is one on human longevity, and I am rapdily nearing the three-score and-ten years mentioned, but by no means guaranteed, in the Bible. At this case's rate of progress it's still going to be on the books when you and I, Jack, are pushing up daisies and Sergeant Evert here will be thinking of putting in his retirement papers.''

Turning slightly to look at Lerch from the passenger seat, Evert said, ''Regarding papers, I've been wading through Rupert's financial records. If he was engaged in cooking the books, Sara Hobart had to be involved because she's the one who kept them.''

Lerch looked at him sidewise. ''Your point being?''

''Well, if Rupert was killed because he was swindling somebody, that could explain both why Sara continued to work for him even though he was no longer interested in her romantically, and why she had to be eliminated.''

Leaning forward again, Nick said, ''The methods of killing don't fit that scenario. His throat was cut. She was strangled. I don't see those methods jibing with simply squaring away a matter of business among thieves. It's more likely they would have been taken out cleanly and quietly with a nice reliable pistol fitted with a silencer. The motive here is personal, which is why I was so easily misled and ended up with egg all over my face in this Wieder charade.''

''Oh cheer up, Nick. Look on the bright side. Who knows what breakthrough we might make when Evert locates the safety deposit box that matches the key Rupert put in the box along with that Nazi officer's ID papers?''

''Assuming he'll be able to find it. The key could very well be for the safe where Rupert stashed the loot while he unloaded it. That key might have been in that cigar box because Rupert saw it as another war souvenir.''

''If that was the case,'' said Evert, ''why direct you to it?''

''He had convinced himself that somehow he was about to have to atone for killing Herr Cap-it-*ahn* Kadiddlehopper. He expected to get his comeuppence on the Sunday he sat up all night with a Luger in his hand. Something had happened to alarm him. Woolley said that when he and Rupert were in Harvard Square he was afraid Rupert was having a heart attack. I think something or someone he saw had scared him. Maybe it was Wieder's brother. All I know for sure is that Rupert was in my store early on Monday morning with a scheme to lure me to his store later that night because he expected trouble. That is also when he left that envelope addressed to me in his locker. By directing me to that chest in the store window he counted on me to connect the items in it to a motive for murder.''

''Which you did.''

''Yes, Jack, I did,'' Nick said as the car cruised past the Necco factory on Massachusetts Avenue, ''and as a result of my muddled logic I made a horse's ass of myself tonight. Now I am going to have to explain myself to a woman who is quite unlikely to let me forget it.''

Entering his apartment to the sounds of his upstairs neighbor's typewriter, Nick looked across the dark living room and saw with relief a green light on the answering machine indicating no messages had been recorded. Flip-

ping a wall switch, he turned on lights and gazed at the
telephone itself.

Torn between his heart's insistence that he call Peg
Baron to explain questioning her about the concert tickets
and his brain's counsel that he would be inviting another
row, he poured a glass of scotch, carried it to a chair, lit
an Upmann, and imposed a truce until morning.

To ensure that Peg could not call him he lifted the
phone's receiver off the hook and settled back in the chair
to sip and smoke in a silence that even Woolley seemed to
sense he needed by ceasing his typing. But when the effects
of the scotch began to be felt and the delicate ash of the
Upmann was achieving a satisfying length, his state of tranquillity was rudely shattered by three loud knocks on the
door.

Deducing the person on the other side of the door could
be no one but Woolley, he shouted, "It's open."

With worn purple robe open to reveal Gordon tartan pajamas, Woolley entered with uncharacteristic reticence. His
eyes shifted in the direction of the bedroom door. "I'm not
intruding?"

Unmoving, Nick chuckled. "I am quite alone, Professor.
Help yourself to the scotch and a cigar."

"Thanks, but I won't be staying that long."

"If you've come to pump me about developments in the
case, I can tell you with absolute certainty that Stanley Rupert's murder had nothing to do with what happened in
Germany."

"Of course not. The killing of Sara Hobart proved that."

Pondering this truth, Nick took a sip and a puff. "Are
you going to stand there by the door, or are you going to
come in, sit down, and tell me what's on your mind?"

Settling onto the couch, Woolley said urgently, "I have
come seeking your good offices."

"Concerning what?"

"I hope to tap into your influence with Jack the Nimble
to gain me access to Rupert's store."

"May I ask what for?"

"As executor of the estate I am under great pressure
from Rupert's heirs. Rex Trevellyan was on the phone this

evening to harrangue me about getting an expert to appraise the contents of the store in preparation for auction.''

Nick examined his scotch glass with all the intensity of a fortune teller gazing into a crystal ball. ''I'm pretty sure,'' he said, ''that the store is still under seal as a crime scene.''

''I told Rex I thought so, but he was adamant. He started talking about hiring a lawyer and suing.''

Nick grunted. ''The twerp didn't waste any time in claiming Rupert's Montecristos, either.''

''I told him I would look into the matter. Can you help me?''

Nick lifted the glass as if making a toast. ''I'll be happy to apprise Lerch of your dilemma, Professor.''

''That's all I ask,'' Woolley said, rising from the couch. ''If he should prove reluctant, feel free to tell him that he can have one of his men present to ensure no one goes out the front door with anything. Or he can have one of his men monitor the process with the store's security camera.''

Nick flinched so violently that ash fell from his cigar to his lap. ''What security camera?''

''The one Rupert had installed after he heard about the theft of your wooden Indian. After I told him of your refusal to allow Craig Spencer to set up a video camera to keep an eye on it, he immediately sent for Spencer to have him install such a system in his store. I thought Craig told you at the time.''

Nick angrily brushed away the ash. ''You thought wrong.''

''Craig not only installed the system,'' Woolley continued as he tied the belt of his robe, ''he persuaded Rupert to engage him to upgrade it from time to time.''

''Spencer always was quick to recognize when he had a good thing going for himself.''

''It is quite the sophisticated apparatus, or as Craig likes to say, state of the art. It uses a hidden TV camera the size of a cigarette package connected to a recording machine with a tape that runs twenty-four hours. That's why the lights were always left burning in the store. The machine is the kind found in a bank. Rather than running continuously like a motion picture it records a series of snapshots of what's going on in the store.''

''Are you certain the system was still being used?''

''Oh yes. Stanley was very keen on the system. The very first thing he did when he went into the store each afternoon was take out the tape from the previous day and put in a new one. He would keep each tape for a week and then reuse it.''

Remembering the tapes in Rupert's office, Nick gave Woolley a withering look and picked up the receiver of the phone. ''I hope that at some point in this case,'' he said, ''there will be no more rabbits pulled out of your hat, Professor.''

''Who are you calling?''

''Jack Lerch, of course. He needs to know about this.''

''Surely his men would have checked the system by now.''

''How can anyone be expected to check what he doesn't know about? You should have mentioned this security system long ago.''

With a dignity unexpected of a man in a robe and pajamas, Woolley strode to the door. ''I assumed that any detective with a modicum of savvy would have expected in this day and age that a store full of valuable antiques would have some sort of system as protection against thieves and shoplifters.''

''When I was in that store I didn't spot any security.''

Woolley opened the door and smiled. ''Is it not the purpose of such a security system to go unnoticed?''

''Do you happen to know where Spencer installed the camera and the tape recorder?''

''As I recall, the latter is on a shelf within a small, red lacquer Oriental chest. The camera is directly above, concealed in an elk's eye. I believe the optic Spencer chose was the left.''

Half an hour later, Lerch again crossed the sidewalk at the front of Rupert's store. ''When this case is wrapped up,'' he said as he unlocked the door, ''I ought to charge

Woolley with impeding my criminal investigation, and possibly obstruction of justice.''

"Do that, Jack,'' Nick said as the door swung open, "and I'll have to take the stand and testify on his behalf as a character witness.''

"He's a character all right,'' Lerch said, flipping a switch to turn on the lights and gazing at the row of stuffed heads on the wall to the right. "He said the camera is in the elk's head?''

"That's correct.''

Lerch sighed and walked toward the heads. "I know you were a city boy like me, but would you by any chance know which of these moth-bitten atrocities is an elk?''

"If I recall correctly from watching nature shows on public television with my grandkids,'' Nick said, "it's the one with the larger antlers and a bigger nose.''

Lerch's examining eyes moved downward from the head. "You must be right, because there's the red cabinet below it.'' Crouching before it, he opened a pair of doors. "And there's a VCR.''

Nick bent and looked at a small green light at the front of the recorder. "It's turned on. Front-loading. If there's a tape in it and you press that button it should pop out.''

"Say a prayer to the god of homicide detectives,'' Lerch said as the cassette ejected, "that this tape was made that Monday.''

"It has to be from that day,'' Nick said. "The store's been sealed since then. Who could have touched it?''

"The killer on his way out?''

"We'll know if it's the right one if I appear on it. Then it's just a matter of seeing who was in the store and left it before I came in at eight-fifteen. How soon do you think we can we take a look at it?''

"Immediately after you phoned me about this,'' Lerch said, pocketing the tape, "I got on the horn to Evert and told him to rustle up the department's best electronics technician and have him standing by at the crime lab. If we find anything useful on the tape, such as a picture of the killer, he'll be able to make a print of it. And if the tape is blurry or out of focus he has computer equipment to enhance it. Science! Ain't it just great? Someday all this electronic wizardry is going to put all the old-fashioned detectives like me out to pasture.''

Two hours later, with an unlit Upmann in his mouth, Nick sat in a chair in front of the cluttered desk in Lerch's smoke-free office, studying a three-quarter profile of a figure in the eight-by-ten, black-and-white print of the image from the videotape. Presently, he asked, ''Are you a gambling man, Jack?''

''I suppose it depends on what the payoff might be.''

''How does catching a killer sound to you?''

''Just fine! But what are the odds on my winning?''

''Fifty-fifty. The risk is that if I am wrong and the story of what I'm asking you to do ever gets out, you could wind up on the street and the City of Cambridge Police Department may end up defending itself in a huge defamation suit.''

Lerch thought a moment, tugged at his jowls, shrugged, and sighed. ''If I weren't a gambling man I would never have applied for a job in homicide. What do you want me to do?''

''I want you to join me in a conspiracy of deception.''

''Sounds like fun.''

''However outrageously mendacious I am, I want you to play along with me.''

''Okay, it's a deal. What is the venue for this game?''

''A house on Beacon Hill.''

# Twenty-eight

"THIS IS A photograph made from a videotape taken from the security system in Stanley Rupert's store. You will note that it also shows the time, day of the week, and date the recording was made. The young man in the picture is shown leaving Rupert's office at a quarter to eight on the night he was murdered. No one else but the man in the picture and your grandfather was in the store in the two hours before. The next person to enter the store was myself at eight-seventeen at which time I found your grandfather dead. The only conclusion to be drawn from this picture and those facts is that the man in the picture killed him. Do you agree that a picture doesn't lie?"

Rex Trevellyan studied the photo. "This one seems to be a bit on the fuzzy side."

"Nonetheless," Nick said, "I'm confident a jury will have no problem recognizing you as the man leaving your grandfather's store at the time and date indicated in the picture."

"If this photo alone proved that I killed my grandfather," said Rex, tossing the photo aside, "you would have arrested me and put me in handcuffs by now."

"You're right," Nick said, retrieving the picture. "It isn't proof by itself. But, as Lieutenant Lerch will tell you, proving you killed Rupert is just a matter of getting the report on the results of the DNA test he had made on the cigar that was found in the ashtray on your grandfather's desk.''

''Well, not a test on the cigar itself,'' Lerch replied, ''but of the DNA that was in the dried saliva on the butt.''

''I'm sure you know what DNA is, Rex,'' Nick said. ''Scientists call it the master code that determines all the things about us—eye and hair color, physique, even our personality traits. DNA is why you look so much like your grandfather, and also why you so stongly resemble your cousin Harry. All that's needed is to compare the DNA found on the cigar butt with DNA extracted from a sample of blood that I'm certain a judge will order you to let a police department doctor draw.''

''If a cigar butt is the basis of your case, gentlemen,'' Rex said, making a show out of taking a cigar from an elegant humidor on the table next to his leather club chair, ''I would say you've got a very serious problem.''

Lerch asked, ''What problem is that?''

''The cigar you had tested for DNA was not mine. It was the old man's. I took my cigar with me.''

Lerch said, ''You admit you smoked a cigar in that office?''

''Of course I admit it,'' Rex said, opening the curved end of the cigar with a silver punch, ''but when I left, grandfather was alive and still smoking. If you found a cigar in an ashtray, it was his cigar.''

Nick slowly shook his head. ''You *thought* it was your cigar that you took with you, but you grabbed Rupert's by mistake.''

Speaking as he lit his cigar, Rex said, ''That is a ludicrous and unprovable allegation.''

''In selling Stanley Rupert nearly every box of cigars he'd smoked in the last fifteen years,'' Nick said, ''I got to know his smoking habits very well. He was one of those cigar aficionados who makes a point of removing the band. You leave the band on.''

''Is that a crime?''

''Unfortunately for you, in your haste to get away that night you picked up Rupert's cigar. The half-smoked cigar we found in the ashtray had a band intact. Both cigars smoked on that night were Montecristo Churchills I sold to Rupert that morning. There is no getting away from the fact that the person who smoked the second Montecristo in that office was Stan's killer. Inasmuch as the security tape shows you as the only person to enter and leave the store between seven and eight-seventeen was you, I believe, and I'm confident Lieutenant Lerch concurs, the evidence that you killed him is compelling."

"I do indeed concur," declared Lerch. "It's more than what the law demands for the district attorney to argue guilt beyond a reasonable doubt."

"This assumes there were no mitigating circumstances," Nick said, "such as acting in self-defense."

Rex snorted a laugh and a plume of smoke. "Self-defense? Against that old man?"

"I take your point, Rex," Nick said. "And the fact that he was killed from behind would also rule out justifiable homicide. I'm not a lawyer, Rex, but I've been involved in a lot of murder cases as a cop. Experience has taught me that there is not much a defendant can do to help himself in such an open-and-shut case as this one except confess. Right, Jack?"

"Confession is not only good for the soul," Lerch said with an emphatic nod, "it can also be a good way to get the sentence reduced so there can be a chance for parole when a man is still young enough to enjoy it."

"Excuse me, gentlemen, but shouldn't someone be advising me that I have the right to remain silent?"

"That applies only if you are arrested," Lerch said. "You're not under arrest. You are correct about the quality of the photo, but that's not going to be anywhere near as important for putting you on trial for murder as the DNA results. Once they are in my hands I might not be in a position to make recommendations to the district attorney based on the amount of cooperation I received in the investigation. It's one thing to go out and place somebody under arrest, and quite another if a suspect realizes the game is over and owns up willingly to what he's done."

Rex regarded the cigar ash. "I'm listening."

"That's why Nick suggested to me that it might be worth

my while to talk with you informally, lay out the evidence, and give you a chance to make a clean breast of it. Of course, if you want to play fast and loose with your future by playing hardball with me, that is both your right and the risk you take. All I can do is advise you that your best chance of striking a bargain with me is right now.''

Rex returned the cigar to his mouth. "How much bargaining room do I have?"

"Frankly, there is not a whole lot either Nick or I could do for you without hearing your confession. You must admit to yourself that the evidence is there in that picture of you."

"The picture is there. It's fuzzy, but it's there. But this stuff about DNA evidence, well, that seems a little farfetched to me. I mean, you guys could have concocted it to trick me into blurting out a confession."

"Yes, we could have done that," Nick said, glancing at Lerch. "In fact, the United States Supreme Court has ruled that police may legally lie to get a confession. But we didn't."

Rex removed the cigar from his mouth, let out a long and pained sigh, and looked at the cigar with a half smile. "I can't believe I grabbed the wrong cigar in that office. As a matter of fact, I can't believe any of this happened." The smile stretched into a grin. "And I'm not sure either of you will."

Nick shrugged. "Go ahead and try us."

Rex thought for a moment, retrieved the cigar, puffed twice to get it going again, and said, "Since you seem to have me dead to rights anyway, why not?"

"Exactly," exclaimed Lerch.

"You could say my killing him was overdue justice."

"Justice for whom?"

"For the man he'd killed, even if it did happen more than fifty years ago and the guy he gunned down was a Nazi war criminal."

Lerch glanced anxiously at Nick. "How did you come to know about that incident?"

Rex sank back in his chair. "Ah, obviously you also know. I am certainly impressed by your detective work."

Lerch snapped, "Cut the crap and answer my question."

With a tenuous smile, Rex said, "How I came to know about it was one of those serendipitous events that can alter the course of one's life. In this case, it happened about four years ago as I was waiting to speak to Grandfather about borrowing money. You see, I was under a lot of pressure regarding gambling debts. Sara Hobart informed me he had just gone out to the bank. While I was waiting in that jumble of junk he called an office, I rummaged in his desk, hoping to find cash. I knew he always kept some stashed somewhere. In a bottom drawer I found an old cigar box. Being a naturally curious person, I gave it a shake. Something rattled around inside. When I opened it, I was disappointed. Instead of money, I found what appeared to be more of the old man's boring war souvenirs. One was the identification document belonging to a German officer. There was also a faded snapshot of four American soldiers, one of whom was obviously my grandfather. And there was a paper, folded. When I read it, I was flabbergasted to find that it was some kind of agreement with four signatures."

Nick nodded. "They called it a compact. May I safely assume you saw it as an answer to your money problems?"

"As I was entertaining that possibility, Sara Hobart walked in and demanded that I put the cigar box back and get out."

"And did you?"

"Pass up the opportunity of a lifetime? Not a chance."

"What did you do?"

"When you were in that office on the night of the mur— on the night granfather got his just deserts, did you happen to see a photocopier?"

"Where's the copy you made of the things you found in the cigar box?"

"I burned them."

"Why kill Sara?"

"That was Harry's doing."

"How did he get involved?"

"He was pressing me for what I owed him. When I paid him off, and continued to settle my gambling debts, he got curious about the source of my newfound wealth. Naturally

I did not confide in him. Unfortunately, a time came when I had to."

"What happened?"

"First, the old man refused to pay anymore. He said he was broke. I said I didn't believe him. He said he didn't care what I thought because someone was out to kill him. I laughed at him. He said if I didn't get out he'd go to the police because he was a dead man anyway."

"So you made that prophecy self-fulfilling."

"Yes."

Nick smiled. "Then Harry tried blackmailing you?"

Rex grunted a laugh. That was a situation I planned to take care of, sooner rather than later."

Lerch asked, "Where is Harry now?"

"He's honeymooning in New York City."

Lerch drew a cell phone from a pocket. "Not for long."

# Twenty-nine

SATURDAY EVENING WAS the quiet dinner Nick had been anticipating with Jean, Mike Tinney, and Peg at the Line-up, a bar and restaurant off Park Square that catered to those who worked in the nearby Boston police headquarters. But somehow the evening had mushroomed into a celebration of the end of the Rupert case.

"We'll be stopping on the way to pick up Peg," said Nick as Woolley settled into the passenger seat of Nick's car.

"I thought she was touring with the pianist."

"She changed her mind."

"Since everything is apparently lovey-dovey between you and Peg once more," said Woolley, "I suppose I shall have to cancel my plans to marry her. But I have no intention of returning the pipe you gave me as a wedding present."

"It's fair compensation for your disappointment."

"I must say I was becoming increasingly alarmed by the way Peg was fawning over Wilhelm Wieder. But now I understand she was using him in an attempt to make you jealous."

Nick snorted a laugh. "That's baloney."

"I have a much longer history with women than you, Nick. I know all their tricks and wiles." He paused and stared at traffic as they moved along Massachusetts Avenue. "I know it's wrong for sins of a father to be visited upon the son, and in this instance the grandsire's to a third generation, but I find it hard to believe Wieder knew nothing of what happened in Ohrdruf Nord."

"We all have demons to deal with, Professor."

"I assume Nimble Jack will be at this soiree."

"Why not? He's got a lot to celebrate. Rex and Harry have signed confessions: Rex for Rupert's murder; Harry for Sara's."

Woolley sighed. "Sara Hobart and Rex were both blackmailers! What a shock that must have been for Stanley."

Nick's tone turned cold. "Yesterday the dogged Sergeant Gary Evert was checking banks where Rupert and Sara did business. We had a key to Rupert's safe deposit box, but there was nothing in it. But not so with Sara's. After Evert obtained a court order to open it, he found it packed with cash and jewelry. One item was a diamond and emerald necklace that no amount of savings from what Sara earned as Rupert's assistant could account for her owning. We won't know its total value until an appraiser examines it. But I will not be surprised if it was part of Kadiddlehopper's loot that Sara claimed for herself. I could be wrong, but Lerch has asked a group that tracks down property stolen by the Nazis to see if the necklace might be on a registry. Lerch is like me. He hates to close out a case without tying up loose ends."

"I assume that he intends to hog the credit for the solution of the murders at the inevitable press conference."

"Why shouldn't he do a little crowing? It was his case."

"Officially. *Unofficially* it was yours, start to finish."

"If you're going to follow that logic," Nick said, "you are the one who should be on the receiving end of kudos. It was you who pointed out the existence of the security system which caught Rex on tape."

"Since you insist on refusing to accept the importance of your role in this affair," Woolley said, "why not assign credit to Craig Spencer? If he had not installed that setup Rex could not have been brought to book."

"If I were to adopt that reasoning I should have assigned credit for the resolution of the case to a certain Harvard law student. If he hadn't arranged the kidnapping of my cigar store Indian fifteen years ago, the subject of installing a security system to keep an eye on it would never have come up, and Craig would not have been hired by Rupert to install one in the elk's head. By the way, how are you doing with the task of liquidating it and the rest of the contents of the place?''

''It proceeds apace. But in pursuance of my responsibilities as executor of the estate I have come across in the files an exchange of letters between Rupert and a man whose great-grandfather was in the tobacco trade during the period of the American Civil War. I think you might be interested in it. He was offering to sell Stanley a rare document which I do believe you should now acquire in order to display it in your store. It would be ideal for you to frame and hang on the wall alongside the Kipling poem.''

''If it's Christopher Columbus's diary, no thanks.''

''In my opinion what this man has is much more interesting. The document is directly related to the history of tobacco merchandising in the United States. It is signed by none other than President Abraham Lincoln.''

''I wasn't aware that Abe was a smoker.''

''I don't believe he was, but the document that was offered to Rupert continues to affect cigar selling. The importance of it is discernible on every box of cigars in stock in your store. To raise funds to finance the Civil War Lincoln imposed a tariff on the sale of cigars by requiring each box of cigars to bear a revenue stamp. This meant imposing standards for packaging. That is why, today, cigars are sold in boxes of twenty-five, fifty, and one hundred. The document Rupert was negotiating to buy is the law Lincoln signed to enact that requirement.''

''That's very illuminating, Professor, but I'm not interested in buying it.''

''Then perhaps another fact related to this item will excite your interest in obtaining it, not in your role as a tobacconist, but as the detective who really solved the Rupert case. It just so happens that Stanley was set to close the deal on the Lincoln document the day after he was murdered. The man who has the paper was scheduled to come to Rupert's shop on Tuesday. Perhaps he can sell it to you.''

Nick smiled. ''Oh, no! To quote Stan Rupert: 'You have no idea how slick forgers are.' ''

Stopping the car in front of Peg Baron's apartment house, Nick was pleased to find her waiting outside.

## *Epilogue*

AT THREE O'CLOCK in the morning, Nick was seated on the couch in the living room of his apartment with his left arm resting lightly on Peg's shoulder and a Dunhill Diamante cigar given to him by Mike Tinney in his right hand.

"What are you thinking about, Nick? The case?"

Stirring, Nick took a puff of the fine cigar. "Nope. I was remembering other police bars I've known through the years."

Peg patted his left knee. "And missing them?"

"Just . . . remembering." As he spoke, hushed voices drifted up from Brattle Street. "Somebody ought to call a cop."

Peg smiled. "It's another Saturday night in a college town."

"Yeah, I guess you're right," Nick said, pushing up from the couch. Going to the window, he said, "But you never know."

"Once a cop," Peg said, "always a cop."

Looking down to the pavement, Nick laughed as he watched two youths struggle toward Brattle Square toting a wooden Indian.